Winter Wonderdach

Cozy Mysteries with a Dash of Dachshund

Alice Kanaka

Table of Contents

More Books by Alice Kanaka

<u>Samantha Olivares Mysteries</u>

The Cardinal & the Crow
The Cardinal, the Fat Boy, & the Flamingo
The Cardinal & the Hawk
The Cardinal & the Crane

<u>Bumfuzzle and Cattywampus: Unlikely Detectives</u>

Trouble at the Buckeye Festival
Mystery at Rutherford Mansion

<u>Standalone</u>

Pious Assassin

Chapter 1
Holiday Blues

Lizzy was in a foul mood. Worse, she felt guilty about it. All the songs and movies told her Christmas should be a time of good cheer. Yet there she sat on a hard wooden bench in the Harperstown police station—stewing.

That morning, feeling depressed by the season and alone in a new place, she decided to take a walk. *Surely the scenic, snow-covered town and the physical activity will make me feel better.* Her plan nearly succeeded. Her eyes lit on the community center, decorated in sparkling red and green, and her spirits began to lift.

What happened next, however, brought them crashing down. One of the town's four 'brilliant' police officers stopped her, accusing her of stealing their community Christmas tree and the gifts beneath it.

"Even if I wanted a tree, which I don't, where would I put it, Sherlock?" she asked, and was promptly arrested.

The officer in question left her on the bench, still in cuffs, and went to get a donut or something. Lizzy was so angry she could almost see the black cloud forming over her head. She closed her eyes and tried to meditate. When she opened them again, and glanced at her watch, two hours had passed. *I must have dozed off. What is taking them so long?*

A tall, muscular man with curly red hair walked out of the back and leaned over the reception counter to retrieve a file. Catching sight of her sitting on the bench, his eyebrows rose. *His eyes are so green.* He approached and asked, "Have you been helped?"

Lizzy held up her cuffed wrists and said, "I've been waiting here for over two hours."

"Who brought you in?"

She shrugged. "The brainiac with the bald head and the scraggly mustache."

"Do you know why?"

"I think it's because I called him Sherlock. I'm afraid I have a bad attitude today."

"Just a moment, please."

⁂

She found it difficult to sustain her anger in the face of his polite professionalism. In fact, her mood was beginning to lift again when he returned with the officer who had arrested her. Then it took another nosedive. The smirk on his face was insufferable. *Moron.*

"Ma'am, this is Officer Nettle. Nettle, could you tell me why you brought her in?"

"She's suspected of theft."

"Theft of what?"

"The community center tree and gifts."

"How did she transport them? It was a twelve-foot tree."

"She must have had an accomplice."

"Mm-hm. With a truck. What made you decide she was responsible?"

"I followed footprints from the door, and she was standing at the end of the walkway."

"Were they a match?"

"Huh?"

"Did the footprints match her boots?"

"I...uh..."

"You didn't check?"

Nettle looked at his feet. "No."

"Okay, so you arrested her and brought her in when? Three hours ago, would you say?"

Looking at his watch, Nettle nodded.

"What have you been doing since then? Have you filed any paperwork?"

"No, Sir."

"Why not?"

"I got a call."

"About the theft."

"Yes."

"So you knew she was innocent, yet left her sitting here in cuffs for hours? Would you say that is a violation of her rights? Dereliction of duty, perhaps?"

Lizzy almost felt sorry for Nettle, but not quite. He was a bully.

* * *

Appalled by Nettle's behavior, Jason removed the young woman's cuffs and instructed his deputy to write a detailed report of the arrest. Then he invited his victim into his office. "I'm Captain Jason Schneider and I'd like to apologize on behalf of the Harperstown police department." He held out his hand for her to shake.

"Thank you," she said, shaking his hand.

"We haven't met. Are you new in town, or just visiting?"

"I just moved here."

He wondered why she didn't supply her name or tell him where she lived but he didn't really have any right to ask.

"How do you like it here, other than your visit to the police station?" He smiled.

"It's okay." She ran a slender tan hand through short blonde hair, making it stand on end. "This is a hard time of year for me. I probably should have waited until the new year."

Again, he wondered. "Aren't you hot?" he asked, eyeing her thick winter coat and heavy snow boots.

"Yes. When I go outside, I'll probably turn into a popsicle."

"Would you like a ride home?"

"No, that's okay. It's not far."

The silence was awkward. "I should go," she said finally. "Thank you for helping me out."

Jason stood when she did and held out his hand again. "It was nice meeting you," he said.

She gave him a wan smile and turned toward the door, but stopped when he asked, "What's your name?"

"Lizzy."

Then she was gone, and he wanted to know more about her. He wanted to see her again.

Lizzy hunched against the icy wind as she walked the two miles home. Captain Schneider had lifted her spirits somewhat, but she was still faced with the upcoming holiday. The old-fashioned shops on Main Street were a constant reminder, decked out with lights and all manner of Christmas paraphernalia. *What's with the candy canes?* They were everywhere. Along the streets, in shops, decorating trees. Stopping in front of the Hummingbird bakery, she waffled. *Is twice a day excessive?* The proprietress, Dottie Peele saw her and waved. Waving back, Lizzy continued walking.

As she crossed the street to her house, sitting on the corner without a decoration in sight, she noted the house on the opposite side of the intersection. *That house looks like it threw up Christmas. At night you can probably see it from space.* Then she thought about her uncharitable attitude. *Am I a grinch? Why should I celebrate losing my family? I hate Christmas.* She thought about the police captain again and sneered. *He looks like someone who's filled with Christmas cheer. Definitely not the guy for me. William was bad enough.* Her selfish ex had been all for receiving gifts on every occasion but rarely gave them in return. He didn't care if she decorated, as long as his pile of presents was waiting on Christmas morning. Lizzy frowned.

I need to get out of my rut. I know. I'll try out my skates. She smiled and let herself into her house.

Despite a lack of heat and hot water, Lizzy loved her new house. The 1900-era Queen Anne was much larger than she needed, but the location was good and the price even better. A construction firm from Sioux Falls had remodeled the downstairs before she moved in. Essentially what she had was an enormous roller rink, sparsely populated with furniture.

Peeling off her snow pants and heavy coat, she stood shivering in shorts and a tank top. *I'll warm up as soon as I get moving.* She retrieved her skates from the closet and sat on the long cream-colored sofa to put them on, pausing to turn on the sound system. Her energy soared as she flew through the house to Michael Jackson, getting faster and more daring as she became familiar with her path. Forward, backward, bouncing and spinning, she found her joy.

The doorbell was her undoing. Surprised, she looked at the door and ran into a small table, arms, legs, and vase in an airborne jumble before crashing to the floor. Lizzy sat amidst the wreckage and said, "Ow." Getting off the floor in roller skates while surrounded by glass, was tricky. The song continued along with the pounding on her door. By the time she got to her feet and shut off the music she was annoyed.

"Yes? Who is it?" she asked from behind the closed door.

"Are you okay?"

"I'm fine. What do you want?"

"I'm Holly. I live across the street. I made a giant lasagna and can't eat it all myself, so I wondered if you'd like to have supper with me."

"I'm sorry. I have a little situation right now but thank you for the offer."

"I have wine too… and homemade brownies."

"Maybe some other time." *Darn. Lasagna sounds good. Too bad it comes with a visitor.*

Resuming her seat on the sofa to remove her skates, Lizzy sighed. *That was really fun.* She wished she hadn't been interrupted and she wished she had hot water. *I need a shower.* The shards of shattered ceramic remained where they fell but they'd have to wait. Once she cooled off, she wouldn't want to get in the cold water. She sprinted up the stairs where she took a quick icy shower and got into her warmest sweatpants and hoodie. Adding socks and slippers to ensure she didn't cut her feet; she went back downstairs to make a cup of coffee and deal with the mess.

Placing a frozen dinner in the microwave, she ambled to her long curved black desk and opened her laptop. The desk sat under a chandelier, where someone else's dining table belonged. Lizzy enjoyed facing the window and French doors so she could look outside as she worked. The microwave dinged and she sat at the kitchen table to eat. *Lasagna would have been better*, she thought as she ate the bland chicken parmesan and soggy green beans. *I should learn how to cook. This stuff is gross.*

After dinner she sat to write. Immersed in her story, all her mundane worries and fears faded away, leaving her content. The hours flew by as she happily crafted a world far different than her own. Shivering, she glanced at the clock and saw it was two in the morning, so she saved her work and trudged upstairs to get ready for bed.

Chapter 2

Visitors

The next morning, Lizzy donned her outerwear and stepped out her front door to find it cleared of snow. *Someone shoveled my sidewalk. That's really nice. I wonder who did it...and when? In the middle of the night?* Her new neighbors baffled her, but she was pleased about the sidewalk, until she tried to descend the front steps at least. They had iced over, and they were very slick. Her feet moved faster than she did, and she ended up on her keister. *My bottom will be black and blue.* Getting on her hands and knees, she crawled to an unshoveled spot and stood. Then she carefully hobbled down the street to the Hummingbird.

Lizzy pulled open the door, breathing in the scents of freshly brewed coffee and pumpkin pie. A healthy-looking poinsettia sat on the counter and a red garland lined glass cases. The half a dozen round tables surrounded by comfortable chairs sported embroidered red tablecloths. Dottie greeted her like an old friend. "Good morning. You're a little late today," she said.

"Yeah. I was up past my bedtime."

"I just took a batch of cranberry-orange scones out of the oven so you can be my taste tester."

"I might be drooling a little." Lizzy grinned. She loved Dottie's nose and was still trying to find a place to use it in her novel. Average-sized, not too big or small, it rose from the bridge in the size and shape of a marble. It should have been ludicrous, but it somehow fit with her pink-tipped white hair and fuchsia lipstick. *It's so unique and gives her loads of character.*

"Have a seat and I'll join you. It's quiet this morning."

Dottie brought two cups of coffee and two scones to her table and sat with her.

Lizzy took a bite of the scone, and her eyes rolled back. Hand over her heart she said, "This might be my new favorite food." The soft warm scone contained chunks of cranberry and orange peel with an orange glaze drizzled on top. It was moist and just sweet enough. She wanted two but didn't want Dottie to think she was a pig.

"Would you like another?" Dottie the mind-reader asked.

Lizzy nodded sheepishly. "They're delicious."

Dottie brought her a second scone and resumed her seat. "How long have you been here now? About a week?"

"Four days."

"Have you made some friends?"

"Just you." Lizzy smiled.

"My husband and I are having a Christmas party at our house this weekend, if you'd like to come. He can pick you up if you need a ride."

She hesitated, wondering if Dottie could see the panic in her eyes. She didn't want friends or social obligations. She just wanted to be left alone. "Can I let you know?"

"Of course. More coffee?"

Before she departed, Lizzy bought some scones, onion bagels, and a loaf of homemade bread, partly out of guilt. *No friends. No parties. Remain anonymous. Finish my manuscript.* She repeated her mantra to herself on the way out the door. *If those crazy paparazzi find me, I'll have to move somewhere else.*

It was snowing again. Lizzy had spent her entire life in Phoenix and the snow made her nervous. She imagined being stuck in her house without food or electricity. Glancing at the small grocery store next to the bakery, she decided to purchase some basic supplies. *What do I need? Candles? Something nonperishable. No, I can just put perishable stuff outside. I wish they'd turn down that music. I can't even hear myself think.* Vaguely annoyed by the Christmas music blaring through the store, she pushed a small cart up and down the aisles. She remembered she had to carry everything home and kept her purchases to a minimum.

The chatty checker, dressed in a crop top and jeans with mile-high hair, became conspicuously silent as she scanned Lizzy's items. The other customers eyed her purchases and whispered amongst themselves. *I need to get home; this is so awkward.* She walked gingerly down the street, careful of the ice, and found a note affixed to her door with duct tape. The note read, "Brought wood. Back porch. Thanks. Bart." *Awesome! I can make a fire. Maybe I won't actually freeze this winter.* Grinning to herself, she dumped her groceries on the kitchen counter and headed for the French doors. She had never seen such an enormous pile of wood, all neatly stacked and ready for use. Not only that, someone, probably Bart, had shoveled a path around the side of the house. Gathering up an armful of wood, she carried it inside and placed it on the little stand next to the fireplace. She stood back and canted her head, wondering how to light it. *I should have bought matches.*

The doorbell rang and she hoped it wasn't the woman with the lasagna again. She approached the door and asked, "Who is it?"

"Dennis Wright. We met the day you moved in."

Lizzy opened the door and looked up. Dennis was a well-proportioned six foot five with short dark-brown hair and an easy smile. "Do you know how to make a fire?"

"Yes, and I know how to put one out," he chuckled.

"That's handy, I guess."

"I'm a fireman."

"Oh. Well, come in, won't you?"

"You bet'cha. Why is it so cold in here?"

"I don't know, but a fire might help. I just got some wood."

"Do you have newspaper or something to use for kindling?"

Paper wasn't a problem, but there was still the matter of matches. "I'll be right back," Dennis said, before leaving the house. When he returned, he carried an unopened box of long matches. "Here we go. One fire coming right up."

"Would you like some coffee?"

"Sure."

Lizzy went into the kitchen to pour them each a cup. The fire that greeted her when she returned with the tray was blazing cheerfully and beginning to take the icy edge off the air.

"How do you like it here so far?" Dennis asked as he sat next to her on the sofa.

"Well, I got arrested this morning."

"What?" He laughed. "What did you do?"

"I might have gotten mouthy with the cop who accused me of stealing the community tree."

"Not Jason?"

"A little bald guy with a mustache. I don't really want to talk about it. Have you lived here your whole life?"

"No. I moved here about five years ago."

"Why? Do you have family here?"

"Yes and no." His face clouded, and he sipped his coffee. "We just met, and I don't know why, but I feel like I can trust you."

Tilting her head to one side, Lizzy waited.

"I haven't told anyone else. In this town, telling one person something is like taking out a newspaper ad."

"You want to keep it quiet."

He nodded. "I'm looking for my dad. I think he got into some kind of trouble. He took off when I was fifteen."

"How old are you now?" Lizzy asked, curious.

"Thirty-five. You?"

"Twenty-eight."

He nodded. "So anyway, five years ago, my mom died and made me promise to find him and give him something."

"You think he lives around here?"

"It's a possibility. My aunt lives here but she won't talk to me. I don't know where else to look."

"Who's your aunt?"

Dennis hesitated. "Ethel Crocker," he said finally.

"She seems to blame my mother for Dad's disappearance. I'm not sure whether she doesn't know where he is, or if she just won't tell me. She's an obstinate woman."

"What if you got a DNA test or something and looked for a match?"

"Wouldn't you have to have some kind of law enforcement connection to do that?"

"Can't you ask the local cops?"

"Schneider hates me. There's no way he'll help."

"Why does he hate you?"

"Hard to say. We've just never gotten along."

Finishing the last of his coffee, Dennis said, "I have to get going. You won't repeat what I told you, right?"

"Of course not. Thanks for helping with the fire. Can I keep the matches?"

"Sure. Thank you for listening." He covered her hand with his and looked into her eyes.

Oh no. Too much sharing. Gently removing her hand, she stood and collected their cups. "Did you say you had another appointment?"

"Yeah. Gotta run. See you later."

⁓

Sitting near the fireplace, wrapped in a fleecy blanket, Lizzy wished she had placed her desk in the living area. She needed to get back to work, but didn't want to leave the fire. The warmth made her sleepy and she dozed off and on, watching gentle snowflakes fall through her front window. Outside, the sky darkened but she felt too lazy to turn on the lights. Neighbors walked their dogs and pre-pubescent boys rode sleds down the street. Her curtainless windows framed life as it unfolded so she sat making up stories in her head about the people of Harperstown. Three of the boys stood together on the corner, one of them pointing at her house.

Then giggling and shoving each other as they crept to her window, they took turns peeking inside until she crawled toward them and surprised them by popping up and making a face. She chuckled as all three boys ran screaming for their sleds.

As she knelt by the window, an elderly man with a cane and a wilted-looking bouquet crossed the street and hobbled up the path to her door. Lizzy vacillated, not wanting company but unable to ignore him after he went to all that trouble. Rising to her feet, she turned on the porch light and opened the door.

"Good evening. I wanted to welcome you to the neighborhood. My name is Theodore Hoffmeyer, but you can call me Theo." He smiled broadly.

"Nice to meet you Theo. I'm Lizzy. Would you like to come in for some coffee or tea?"

"I don't want to intrude…"

"You're not intruding." *Why did I say that?*

"Thank you, then. A cup of tea would hit the spot." He shuffled into the kitchen behind Lizzy, where she pulled out a chair and helped him remove his coat. Once he was seated, she heated a cup of water and took a box of tea bags from the cupboard. "Would you like a scone?"

Declining the scone, he talked non-stop while she made the tea. He spoke of his days teaching high school and his wife who had died twenty years ago, and asked Lizzy about herself.

"What brings you to Harperstown? Do you have family here?"

"No. I came across it when I was looking at charming small towns on the internet, and I found this house for sale and well it was kind of a happy accident."

"Do you like to play cards?"

"Now and then."

"I brought a deck. How about a game of gin?"

Lizzy said, "I don't know how to play. How about blackjack?"

"Sure. One of these days I'll teach you to play gin."

After a couple of hours, Lizzy was beginning to tire from the effort of prolonged socializing. "This has been fun," she said, "but I'm beat. Perhaps we can do it again another time."

"Of course. Thank you for your hospitality. I manage to keep myself busy, but I get a little lonely sometimes. It was nice of you to invite me in."

She sighed and leaned against the front door after he left. She had started across the house toward her desk when a noise made her glance at the French doors. The pale face pressed against the glass stood out clearly in contrast to the darkness beyond. Lizzy screamed and screamed, unable to stop, even after the face disappeared. Switching off the lights so whoever was outside couldn't see in, she worked on slowing her breathing. *It's probably those kids getting me back.* She shivered. *I need to get some curtains.*

Chapter 3

What Does he Want?

A loud rumble from her midsection reminded Lizzy she hadn't eaten since breakfast. She slipped her debit card into her coat pocket and let herself out of her front door, heading for Dave's Diner. *I wonder why the wind is always going the opposite direction. My nose is frozen.*

Warm light poured out of the diner's sizeable plate glass windows and Lizzy's mouth watered at the delicious scent of grilled beef. She pulled the door open and was struck by a barrage of sound; clinking dishes and happy voices raised to be heard over blaring Christmas music. Taking a seat at the bar, she glanced around. Colorful posters and neon signs competed with strands of Christmas lights and garlands. The black and white checkered floor, Formica tabletops, and red upholstered chairs lent the diner a 50s vibe.

The harried middle-aged bartender, wearing a button-down shirt with the sleeves rolled up, stuck a pencil behind his ear and asked, "What can I get you?"

"A Long Island iced tea and a menu please."

"Coming right up." He handed her a menu and moved away to make her drink.

Surprised when Dennis sat on the stool next to hers, she turned.

"Fancy seeing you here."

"A girl's gotta eat. Have you had dinner?"

"You mean supper." He grinned. "Yes. I had something at home."

"This menu is ridiculous. What should I get? What's chislic?"

"You don't want that. Try the hot beef."

"Is that spicy?"

"No, you'll love it."

The bartender placed her tea in front of her and took her order, then asked Dennis what he'd like to drink.

"I'll have whatever she's having."

He walked down to the kitchen window to place Lizzy's order and Dennis asked, "What *are* you having?"

Lizzy laughed and told him but then frowned when he slung his arm around her shoulders. "Let's not go there, okay?"

"Sorry. Just being friendly."

"My last relationship was a train wreck and I'm not looking for another."

"Winter has a way of changing people's minds." He waggled his eyebrows.

A woman with brown, 80s hair and a low-cut top inserted herself between their bar stools and turned her back to Lizzy. "Hey lover," she purred. "I haven't seen you for a while." She leaned in and ran her fingers through Dennis' hair.

Brushing her hand away, he said, "Hey Stace. How's it going? Have you met Lizzy?"

Stacy turned slowly, oozing displeasure.

I wish he hadn't done that. Now I have an enemy.

"You stole the presents from the community center, right?" Stacy spoke loudly, so everyone could hear her. "You got arrested."

"I didn't steal anything."

"That's what they all say," she sneered. "I bet the next time I see you will be on the front page." Turning to Dennis she said, "Give me a call when you're done slumming." She walked away with a slow roll of her hips and was soon surrounded by a group of curious sycophants, eager to hear her story.

Dennis didn't apologize. Instead, he grinned and said, "Look. Your hot beef is here."

Taking a bite, Lizzy thought it was good, something like a sloppy joe, but she'd lost her appetite. "Could I get this to go?"

"Sure. I'll bring you a container."

"And the bill, please."

Dennis offered to walk her home, but she declined. She'd had enough of Dennis Wright for one day. The suspicious eyes of her fellow diners followed her to the door, and she was anxious to escape.

The sandwich was cold and soggy. Heating it in the microwave didn't help. Lizzy left it on the kitchen table and sat at her desk. She opened her laptop, then closed it again. Turning on her stereo, she tried singing as she organized the books on her bookshelves. *What's the matter with me? Here I am with loads of space, and I feel claustrophobic. A small apartment in a big city would've been more practical. What was I thinking?* She paced back and forth. *I'll just go to bed. I'll feel better in the morning.*

Trudging upstairs to her room, she sighed and wrinkled her nose. *I wish I'd had them remodel the bedrooms too. They're so creepy. At least I brought my own bed.* The house came with heavy dark furniture the agent had called antique. *Antique. How about old and needs to be replaced?* Lizzy kept the bedroom doors closed and only visited the outdated bathroom and the room across the hall, the one she chose for herself. Somewhat sleep deprived since she had moved in, she was exhausted and fell asleep almost as soon as her head hit the pillow.

Several hours later she was awake again. She pulled her blankets over her head and squeezed her eyes shut. Listening intently, she knew she was being irrational but couldn't repress her fear. *It's an old house. Old houses make noise.* She listened again. *What could sound like footsteps? Is someone in here? Maybe I should get a burglar alarm.* She kept her eyes closed and tried to imagine herself at the beach, the warm sun on her face, the crash of the waves rolling in, the smell of salt water. *Why did I choose Harperstown of all places? I could have gone anywhere.* She knew why though. No one would ever look for her here. She flung the covers off and got up. Shivering, she turned on the light and checked the thermostat. *Twenty degrees.*

Back in Phoenix it never got that cold. Sweatpants and a hoodie helped a little, but a heater would work better. She went downstairs to make a fire. She followed Dennis' instructions and once she got it going, she started a pot of coffee, taking a sniff of the rich ground medium roast before scooping it into the filter basket. Doing jumping jacks in front of the fire while it brewed, she glanced at the clock and sighed. *Only two o'clock.*

Once the coffee was ready, she carried a cup to her desk, where she turned on her laptop and sat to write. Her eyes gradually closed of their own accord, as her hot desert setting iced over, and her main character shivered. When Lizzy jerked upright, she swiped the moisture in the corner of her mouth with her sleeve, wondering how long she'd been sleeping. Sunlight poured through the windows, warming the house. She looked around and smiled. Even though she hadn't finished remodeling, the construction crew had removed the ratty shag carpet covering natural maple floors, dark dated wallpaper, and wood paneling. Taking out unnecessary walls and painting the remaining ones white, they created a bright open floor plan. *My roller rink.* Cheerful green curtains in the kitchen and throw pillows in primary colors, along with a profusion of houseplants made her feel more at home. *I hope they don't freeze in here.* She gently stroked a leaf.

Having stocked up the day before, she didn't need to visit the Hummingbird, which had become a morning ritual. Instead, she toasted herself an onion bagel and reheated her coffee, considering how she would spend her day. *I need a schedule, and I need to stick to it.* Before William left her, before the mayhem began, she got up when he did. She wrote all day and went to dinner with him when he returned in the evening. One night he didn't come home. She still remembered their final conversation. "I've found someone else," he had said. He called her a lazy boring freeloader. *I wasn't boring. You were. And I paid for half of everything.* Her mouth turned downward but then she laughed. The joke was on him. A month after he left her book took off. Then there was the movie deal.

Enough of that. She shook her head. *A schedule. It's hard to keep a schedule when people are constantly stopping by. And the snow. And having to eat. I'll start small. At least I can plan a sleep schedule.* She had the best of intentions. Determining she should go to bed between ten and twelve, she would rise after eight hours and keep her work schedule flexible. *That's a start.* She nodded emphatically and headed upstairs to brush her teeth.

Her toothbrush was missing. *That's weird.* Brow furrowed, she opened the spare she kept in her cabinet and brushed. Then she wandered through the house looking for anything else out of place. Her keys weren't on the hook by the door. They were on the kitchen counter. *Maybe I did that.* Her toothbrush was in the refrigerator. *What was in that Long Island? I must have been really loopy.*

Once she settled at her desk, she wrote until dinner time. Then she made a sandwich and roller skated—more cautiously than before. Stimulated by her break, she went back to work, forcing herself to stop at her self-imposed bedtime.

❧

Locking her bedroom door, Lizzy took her 9-millimeter Hellcat Pro out of her safe and placed it in her bedside drawer next to her flashlight. *Just in case.* As usual, she fell asleep quickly, waking only when a loud crash sounded from the third floor. *Ghost or person?* She took a deep breath to calm herself. *I have three choices: I can pretend nothing's wrong and hide under my covers, I can call the police, or I can search the house. The smart thing to do would be to call the police, but I've never claimed to be smart. I have the gun. Should I turn on the lights as I go, or leave them out? Lights. Definitely.*

Rising quietly and taking her gun and flashlight out of the drawer, Lizzy moved swiftly to the door and flicked the light switch. Nothing happened. *Is the power out?* Heart pounding, she unlocked the door and stepped into the hall, pointing the flashlight in one direction, then the other.

She crept toward the staircase and swung the beam around the downstairs. Then she shone it back the way she had come. Moving as silently as she could, she made it down four steps before she froze at a piercing high-pitched squeal. When she aimed the light at her feet, she saw a fat rubber chicken with a long skinny neck. *What on earth? Where did that come from?* Wobbling slightly, she grasped the banister. The desire to sit down was strong, but she needed to get downstairs. Feeling a gust of frigid air, she thought again of ghosts as she made her way to the kitchen, where she tried another switch. *Nothing. Now what? A fire?* She felt the icy draught again and swung her flashlight toward the French doors. *Why are they open? Someone's in here.*

Terrified and realizing she had left her phone upstairs; she ran outside and scanned the neighborhood. The lights were on in the house on the opposite corner. Lizzy put her gun in her pocket and the flashlight on the porch before running toward the house. She slid on the ice and lost a slipper in the snow. Landing on her knees, she scrambled to her feet and continued to the front door. Shivering from cold and fear, she glanced over her shoulder at her house and rang the bell. A death knell resounded. She banged on the door until a young woman who looked about her age opened it and peered at her with raised eyebrows.

"There's someone in my house. Can I borrow your phone?"

"Sure. Just a minute." She paused. "Don't you have one?"

"I left it upstairs."

"Come inside. You must be freezing." She let Lizzy in and closed the door. "I'll be right back."

Lizzy waited, trembling.

The young woman strode through a stone arch with her cellphone. Vaguely interested in the home's interior, Lizzy accepted the phone and dialed 911. She reported the intruder before returning it.

"Thank you," she said. "You're a life saver."

"I'm Holly, by the way. The person who offered you lasagna the other day."

"Thank you for that too. That was kind of you. I'm sorry I was occupied." Filled with guilt and a little hungry, Lizzy left the house and went home to wait for the police. She stood on the corner in one slipper, the wet knees of her pants frozen solid, and wished she had thought to grab her coat on the way out.

Jason groaned and rolled over when Serj Tankian's voice blared from his phone. The first line from *Chop Suey* was a rude awakening. "Schneider," he answered sharply.

The dispatcher spoke clearly, with careful enunciation. "Home invader reported at 489 Main Street, the old Pederson place."

"Got it. I'll be there in five." He dressed quickly and released Harvey from his kennel, taking an extra minute to secure his harness and let him do his business.

When he pulled up to the curb, Jason was surprised to see Lizzy standing outside with wide eyes, her short blonde hair standing on end and a gun in her right hand. "We meet again. Is that loaded?" he asked.

She stared at him, mute, then looked at the gun in her hand. "Yes."

He held out his hand and took it, making sure the trigger safety was on before sticking it in the back of his waistband. "What's going on here?" Harvey tried to give her a sniff, but Jason said, "Sit." The giant German Sheppard was unpredictable and had been retired from service after a drug bust went wrong. Jason had adopted him and knew Harvey always had his back, but he kept a firm grip on his lead. Guns were one of his triggers.

Lizzy shook violently, her teeth chattering. "Someone was upstairs, and the lights are out. The back door was open."

Scanning the dark interior of the house over her shoulder, Jason asked, "Is the intruder still inside?"

"I don't know. I might have freaked out a little and ran across the street to use my neighbor's phone." She pointed. "The lights were on."

"Where's yours?"

"Upstairs."

"Let's start by getting your lights on. Do you want to stay out here or come with me?"

"Can I come? I don't want to be alone."

"Stay behind me. Where's your breaker box?"

She stared at him.

"You have a basement, right? Where's the entrance?"

"There's a door under the stairs. I haven't been down there." She followed so closely that they collided when he stopped to open the door. Harvey growled softly. "Sorry." The wooden steps descended into darkness. She backed up.

⸺⸺⸺ ·•◦⊰∞⊱◦•· ⸺⸺⸺

"Come on. Take my hand. It's okay."

Lizzy reluctantly took his hand and shivered. Following him into the abyss, she imagined herself the heroine in a horror movie, making the most illogical choice possible.

"Could you hold the flashlight for me so I can see what I'm doing?"

She took it with shaky hands, and he had the lights restored in seconds. He looked around before approaching the water heater. "Did you know your pilot light is out?"

He really is attractive, Lizzy thought, then firmly shoved that idea out of her head. She had heard of a pilot light, of course, but she couldn't for the life of her remember what it was or why it was important. She stared at him vacantly and he shook his head.

"Didn't you wonder why you didn't have hot water or heat?"

"I did. Yes."

"Come take a look at the water heater. See in there? There should be a little flame."

Lizzy bent down to see where he was pointing and convulsed. Feeling the heat emanating from him she realized she was freezing. "How do you light it if it goes out?"

"It shouldn't go out. Someone probably extinguished it while the house was vacant. But if it does go out for some reason, you can use one of these long matches to relight it." He picked up a dust-covered box of fireplace matches and demonstrated.

"Thank you. I've felt like I'm camping in the arctic tundra. Not that I've ever tried that."

He nodded and glanced at her bare foot. "Where's your other slipper?"

"I lost it."

"Let's go back upstairs and make sure he's gone. Maybe you can grab some dry socks on the way. You must be freezing." Jason led her through the bedrooms on the second floor, letting Harvey check under the beds and in the closets. As he approached the base of the third-floor staircase, Lizzy hung back. "Come on. You'll never feel safe if you don't see for yourself." he said.

"Do you think I should get a burglar alarm? Someone must have a key."

"Or know how to pick locks. It might not be a bad idea."

"I wonder what they want."

"Hard to say." He held out his hand again.

Once upstairs, Jason turned on the light. The unfinished floor was full of the Pedersons' belongings. Boxes that had been neatly stacked and labeled were open and strewn around, their contents spilling onto the ground.

"He was pretty quiet considering the mess he made. He must have dropped something because the bang woke me up.

"What happened to the people who lived here?"

"They both passed away and didn't leave wills. Their only remaining family member didn't want to deal with it."

Chapter 4

Enter Mavis

Jason finally left, and Lizzy collapsed on the sofa. She was just drifting off to sleep when she thought she heard a scratching sound. She sat up and listened, a chill running down her spine. The noise seemed to be coming from the hall closet. *What's in there? Is the intruder still here? More scratching.* Pressing her lips together, needing to know but not sure she wanted to, she picked up the gun Jason had returned and tiptoed to the closet. She took a deep breath and aimed the gun, then yanked the door open. No one was there, but her eye caught movement at her feet as a small reddish-brown football waddled by. Following at a distance, she wondered if it was some kind of regional vermin. It walked into the kitchen and sniffed in the corner, then turned enormous brown eyes in her direction.

"Aurohroher," it said.

"You're a dog."

"Roherer."

"And you talk. Sort of." Lizzy studied the animal and decided it must be a wiener dog. A dachshund. "You should go home. I don't have anything to feed you." She paused. "How did you get into the closet? Is this yours?" She picked up the rubber chicken she stepped on early in the morning.

The dog barked twice and sat, eyes imploring. It was skinny and dirty. "Let's go see the vet. He'll know what to do." She tried to pick the dog up, but it danced away from her and headed for the stairs.

"No. You should stay down here."

The dog ignored her. Grabbing her phone, she looked up the number for the animal clinic across the street and dialed.

"Schneider Pet Clinic," a voice answered.

"This is Lizzy Horn, across the street. I need your help. There's a brown furry thing in my house, and it won't leave. I think it's hungry."

"I'll be right there. Is it a dog or a cat?"

"A small dog."

"I'll bring food."

Not two minutes had passed before Lizzy heard knocking at the door. The woman whose phone she had borrowed the night before carried a doctor's bag, dog food, and a bowl. "Where's the dog?" she asked when Lizzy opened the door.

"I don't know. It went upstairs. Wait. You're the vet?"

"I am." The woman, Holly if Lizzy remembered correctly, smiled and walked into the kitchen, opening the food as she went, and began pouring it into the ceramic bowl. Recognizing the distinct sound the kibble made as it fell into the bowl, the dog hopped down the stairs like an acrobat and raced into the room, barking and wagging its tail.

"Mavis. Is that you? Where have you been?" Holly spoke to the dog, who wagged her tail but didn't stop wolfing down the food.

"Mavis?"

"She's a character. She belonged to the Pedersons, but she disappeared at the same time Mr. Pederson did. I wonder where she's been."

Once Mavis finished eating, her whole body wiggled as she wagged her tail and alternated between Holly and Lizzy, looking for pets. Lizzy tried to pet her, but she kept lifting her long, pointy nose and trying to lick her hand. Then she rolled onto her back and whined. Running her hand over Mavis' little belly and her tiny paw, she was surprised when the paw was rapidly withdrawn.

"She's never liked anyone messing with her paws," Holly said. Opening her doctor's bag, she withdrew a thermometer and a stethoscope. "I'll just give her a quick checkup while I'm here."

"Aren't you taking her?"

"Goodness no. If I started doing that, I'd have hundreds of animals. You should adopt her. She's an excellent guard dog and she'll keep you from being lonely."

"Yeah. She's terrifying."

"She might not be scary, but she's noisy. If anyone comes over, she'll bark her head off."

"I don't really want a pet. I have enough trouble taking care of myself."

"She's wonderful. Just give it a try."

Lizzy sighed.

"She's passed her checkup, but she's malnourished. I'll bring you some supplies after I close for the day, including some high nutrient food. Make sure she has plenty of water and don't overfeed her. She's little but she loves to eat. Just give her one scoop twice a day. You can add a little table food and some warm water if you want to make a gravy, but if you do that, count on doing it all the time; she's liable to refuse her food without it."

"What about going potty?"

"Take her out on a regular schedule. I'll bring a harness and a leash. First thing in the morning, after meals, before bedtime, and whenever she scratches at the door. She's good about letting you know—or she used to be. Oh, here's some dog shampoo. She needs a bath. I'll give her some flea and tick drops this evening once she's clean."

Holly left and Lizzy was alone with Mavis. She had no idea what to do with a dog. "I need a nap. How about you?"

Mavis barked once, a surprisingly robust, medium-pitched woof, and wagged her tail.

"We should give you a bath first. How do I even do that? The sink? The shower? We'll have to figure it out because you're filthy." She headed upstairs and the dog followed, her tail still wagging.

There must be a better way. Lizzy had filled the bathtub with four inches of warm water and plopped Mavis in the tub.

She jumped around, biting at the water, then gave herself a vigorous shake. Lizzy was soaked by the time the little dog was clean, but she wrapped her in a thick towel and dried her as well as she could. She set the dog, still wrapped in the towel, on her bed and changed into dry clothes. To her surprise, Mavis burrowed into the towel and fell asleep. "We should both take a nap, puppy. I'm exhausted."

"Aurohroher." Lizzy opened her eyes to find Mavis staring at her, her long nose only a few inches away.

"What is it, girl?"

Barking twice, Mavis nudged her hand.

Lizzy sat up and placed her on the floor. She ran to the door and back again, barking. "You probably have to go outside, is that it?" Following the little dog downstairs, she opened the door and Mavis shot past her across the porch and down the steps. She burrowed through the snow, popping up again next to the large fir tree that grew in the middle of the yard. Quickly finding a good spot, she squatted and remained in position for twenty seconds. Lizzy counted. "That was a big one. You must've really had to go." Ignoring her, Mavis burrowed back to the sidewalk and trotted to the door. Lizzy sighed. "You're not clean anymore. I guess I'll have to clear a little area for you." She built a fire and wondered what time it was, glancing at the clock on her laptop as she settled down to write.

The frantic barking began a second before the doorbell rang. Lizzy straightened and banged her head on the inside of the refrigerator. She was rubbing the sore spot as she opened the front door.

"I told you she was a good guard dog." Holly was burdened with packages.

"She's going to give me a heart attack. What do you have there?"

"I'm a dog spoiler. I'm almost certain that's why my pet shop never makes a profit."

"I'm happy to pay for supplies. How much do I owe you?"

"Nothing at all, but you can eat with me. I brought the lasagna back."

"You're persistent." Lizzy laughed. "If you brought the brownies we have a deal."

"I did. You were pretty distracted last night. My name is Holly in case you forgot."

"I'm Lizzy. You've rescued me twice now, three times if you include the brownies."

Lizzy turned and strolled back into the house, leaving Holly to follow. She walked to her desk, bending to scribble a note and save her manuscript. Then she closed her laptop and headed for the kitchen, where Holly was unpacking shopping bags and Mavis was bouncing around at her feet. "Sorry about that," she said.

"I think I should be the one apologizing. I didn't mean to interrupt your work."

"It's okay. Sometimes I get so immersed it's hard to pull myself away. I didn't mean to be rude." She ran her fingers through her hair making it stand on end.

"What type of work do you do? And where do you keep your plates?" Holly turned in a full circle, glancing at the cupboards.

"I'm an accountant." She grabbed a bottle of wine before retrieving plates, forks, and wine glasses. Then she placed them on the table and peered over Holly's shoulder. "What all do you have there?"

Extracting a dog bed and blanket, harness and leash, winter coat, toys, special food, flea and tick drops, and a Santa costume, she saw Lizzy staring and grinned. "What? It's almost Christmas. Speaking of which, you should come to the Ball."

"It's kind of you to invite me but I'd rather not."

"Come on. I understand if you don't like to socialize, but everyone needs friends."

Lizzy sighed. *Here I go, getting sucked in again.*

"I don't even have a dress."

"Don't worry. I have dozens. You can take your pick."

"Let's eat. I haven't been working much for the last two days and I still have to clean up the mess upstairs."

"What mess?"

Lizzy told her about the former owners' belongings.

"I can help if you like. I'm still on call over the weekend but the clinic is closed."

"Okay. If you really don't mind. I'll leave it for now and try to get some work done."

Lizzy was amazed by how much Holly looked like the old her, before she altered her appearance. She didn't look like that anymore, but the long wavy brown hair, brown eyes, small nose, curvy body type, everything. They could have passed as sisters. Engrossed in her observation, she ate half her lasagna before she realized Holly was talking to her. "I'm sorry. What?"

"I asked if you like the lasagna."

"Yes. It's delicious. You made it yourself?"

"I did. I love to cook."

"Did you make the brownies too?"

Holly nodded.

"I'll probably have to learn to cook if I don't want to eat at Dave's every day."

"I can help if you like."

"Be careful; I might take you up on that."

"I wouldn't mind at all. What brings you to Harperstown?"

"Peace and quiet. I wanted somewhere I could have uninterrupted time to work."

"Uh oh. I'm feeling guilty again."

"Well, I *do* have to eat, and you *did* make brownies, so I'm not too upset." Lizzy laughed.

Mavis sat staring at them intently as they ate, hoping for a handout. When ESP didn't work, she said, "Ahroorohoh."

"I guess it's your dinner time too," Lizzy said. Just be patient and I'll mix a little lasagna in."

Mavis gave a sharp bark but remained at attention.

"Where did you live before?" Holly asked.

"California. It's a lot warmer there. The policeman who came last night told me the pilot light was out. It was twenty degrees in here."

"You poor thing! And you were outside without a coat."

"I thought I'd never get warm."

"Have you noticed anything strange about this house?"

"Like what?"

"I don't know—like ghosts? People say it's haunted."

"How would they know? Do they come inside?"

Holly shrugged. "They're just rumors."

"I don't believe in ghosts." *Aren't I sounding brave.* Lizzy remembered wondering about the footsteps. "Do you?"

"Maybe. I believe in angels. Do you have insomnia?"

"No. I usually sleep well. Why?"

"I just wondered why you're up so late."

Lizzy set her wine glass down with a thunk and stared at her. *What do you want? Are you some kind of stalker?*

The flush that began in Holly's cheeks and spread across her face and neck was fascinating. She started talking fast, trying to explain herself. *This would make a great scene.*

"I have insomnia. I'm up a lot at night. I wander around either inside or outside if the weather permits. It's dark so I notice when the lights are on. That's all."

Writing the scene in her head, Lizzy forgot all about their conversation. She stared off into space playing out her characters' dialogue.

Holly, on the other hand, was stuck in the present, worried she had already alienated her new friend. Her explanation trailed off and she sat watching Lizzy. She took several sips of her wine as she waited. "Lizzy?" she whispered. Then receiving no response, she said it louder.

Starting, her eyes widening, Lizzy focused on her. "Sorry. Hold on." She rushed over to her desk and grabbed a notebook, scribbling furiously. Then she set it down and casually strolled back to the table. "That was a good one."

"A good what?"

Lizzy blinked. "Um. A good solution to a client's dilemma. I had to write it down so I wouldn't forget it."

"You're not mad?"

"About what? Oh. Of course not. Can we have brownies now?"

Holly nodded and rose to get them from her canvas bag, shaking her head. *I wonder if I made a mistake. She's so strange.* "Why don't we take Mavis for a little walk after supper? I can introduce you to the neighbors."

Lizzy groaned.

"Seriously, you need to make some friends. Plus, they'll make up wild stories about you if you don't get out and meet them."

They finished their meal, and she showed Lizzy how to mix Mavis' food. Mavis stood at their feet, dancing on her back legs but when Lizzy set the bowl down, she didn't eat. She sat in front of the bowl and looked up at her, thwacking the floor with her tail.

"Why aren't you eating?"

"I think she wants a little pet first."

Lizzy bent over and stroked Mavis' head and ears then watched her take a bite. "She's a little dictator."

After Mavis ate, Holly helped get the wiggly dog in her coat and harness and they headed out for their walk.

Chapter 5

Out and About

Mavis pranced down Main Street in the opposite direction from downtown and stopped to sniff a mound of snow.

"Keep that little beast out of my yard."

"Hello Mrs. Crocker," Holly said. "Don't you remember Mavis?"

Ethel Crocker frowned at Mavis and tossed her blonde bob. "Is she back? She was always digging up my garden." Lizzy noticed Ethel hadn't made much of an effort to decorate, just rows of three-foot tall candy canes on either side of the walkway leading to her front door.

"Hello Mr. and Mrs. Fickle," Holly said.

The Fickles, who had been politely listening to Mrs. Crocker's diatribe, were elderly and looked painfully thin, even bundled up in thick winter coats. "Hello, dear," Mrs. Fickle said with a smile. "Who's your friend?"

"This is Lizzy. She lives right next door and Mavis decided she wanted to come home."

One ear rose when Mavis heard her name, and she approached Mrs. Fickle, barking and wagging her tail.

"Oh yes, I remember this one. Such a sweet puppy." Mrs. Fickle's long gray braid fell over her shoulder as she bent to pet Mavis, who was intrigued by the colorful skirt swirling around her boots. Lizzy had seen her peering over the fence, but they hadn't met. Mr. Fickle helped his wife straighten when she was finished gushing over Mavis.

"Nice to meet you Lizzy. What brought you to Harperstown? Do you have family here?"

"Nice to meet you too. My husband passed away and I wanted a fresh start. So far Harperstown seems perfect."

"Just you wait until you've been snowed in for months. I hope you have plenty of wood," Mrs. Crocker said.

"Stop scaring the girl, Ethel," Mr. Fickle said. He smoothed his thick mustache and frowned.

"Ethel's a widow too," Mrs. Fickle said, her sudden smile showing a crooked front tooth. "Perhaps you two can keep each other company."

Mrs. Crocker snorted and crossed her arms across her ample chest. "Just keep that mutt away from me and we'll be fine."

"Let's go, dear. I must get supper started." Mrs. Fickle took her husband's arm. "We're on your other side. Stop by anytime you like," she told Lizzy, "and feel free to bring Mavis."

"Lizzy works a lot, but she'll be at the Christmas Ball."

"Bunch of nonsense," Mrs. Crocker said.

"Has anyone decided what we should do about the presents?" Mrs. Fickle asked.

"The mayor bought another tree and asked everyone who could to bring a replacement gift," Holly said. "The police are hoping they can find the thief and recover the gifts, but Jason said they aren't very optimistic."

"I heard your friend was arrested for the theft," Mrs. Crocker said smugly.

Holly just smiled. "We'll see you all later." Glancing at Lizzy, she began walking down the sidewalk. All too glad to escape Mrs. Crocker, Lizzy gave Mavis a little tug and followed. As soon as they were out of earshot, Holly said, "Ethel Crocker is a little...difficult. And she loves to gossip. It's good you met her. That doesn't mean she won't make up stories about you, but it'll help. How did your husband die?"

"I've never been married but my ex dumped me right before I moved."

"What a crumb. Why did you really choose Harperstown?"

"I just did a search for small towns, and it came up.

"I'm starting to worry about the long winter though."

"I'll help you get stocked up in case of a blizzard and I'm just kitty corner. You should get a snowmobile."

"What do people buy for gifts? I should buy something, right?"

"Anything really. People spend what they can afford, usually something between twenty and forty dollars. I'll let you in on a little secret. Some of us buy more expensive, practical gifts and we draw a tiny little star on the gift tag. Those gifts are given to families who are going through hard times. I usually buy gifts in Sioux Falls or from Amazon, but time is getting short."

"I have no idea what *practical* means for people here. Could you help me?"

"Of course."

After a walk around the block, Holly went home, giving Lizzy her phone number in case she needed anything.

Lizzy spent the evening working on her manuscript then took Mavis outside to do her business and went to bed. At some point in the middle of the night, she decided having a dog must be like having a baby. Mavis wanted on the bed. Then she wanted down. Every time she wanted something she whined, and if that didn't work, she spoke and nudged. She wanted out of the room, then she wanted back in. Her frantic barking at two a.m. had Lizzy cursing under her breath. "Why? Why, why, why?" Then, once fully awake, she unlocked her safe and retrieved her gun. Someone was in the house again. She cracked her door open, and Mavis shot past her, hopping down the stairs. Her barking faded until Lizzy had to strain to hear it. *Where did she go? Is the door open again?* She tiptoed downstairs in time to see the little dog prancing back through the open door, clearly proud of herself. She laid a winter glove at Lizzy's feet and wagged her tail. "Thank you, puppy. We're going to have to do something about that lock. For now, let's go back to bed."

The next morning, Lizzy walked into the Hummingbird with Mavis. Dottie came around the counter and squatted down to pet her. "What a lovely little girl," she said, scratching her ears. "I see you've got her all bundled up."

"Holly gave her the coat. There's a bit of a learning curve."

"I suppose there is. What can I get for you this morning?" Dottie went back behind the counter and washed her hands.

"Coffee and one of those chocolate croissants please. No, make that two."

"Have you worked your way through everything you bought last time?"

"Almost. I had to share." Lizzy grinned.

"Ethel Crocker was in earlier spouting some nonsense about you causing mayhem in the neighborhood."

"Hm. I heard she was quite the gossip."

"An understatement. Here you are. I packed it to go because the shop's busy this morning and not all my customers are animal lovers." She winked.

"I understand. I'm new to this pet thing and didn't want to leave her home alone yet."

"No problem. Steve and I are having supper at Dave's this evening if you'd like to join us, and the diner's dog friendly."

"What time?"

"Around six."

"Sounds good. I'll feed this little eating machine before we go."

⁕

Making another fire and retrieving Mavis' bed, Lizzy said, "Okay, you have a little nap while I write." She looked up once to see Ethel Crocker's face pressed up against the French doors, her hands cupped on either side to block the glare. She stood and walked toward the doors, but Ethel made a speedy getaway.

Mrs. Fickle watched her go before sinking down behind her fence. Shaking her head, Lizzy went into the kitchen to brew a pot of coffee and returned to her desk. She was making decent progress and hoped to have the first draft done by the end of January. She stared out the window, thinking about all her recent distractions. Life in Harperstown was livelier than she had anticipated. Getting up again to pour herself some coffee once it was ready, she looped back to her desk and told herself to stop procrastinating.

When five o'clock rolled around, Mavis looked up at her and said, "Arooerer."

"It's dinner time, isn't it. Let's get you something to eat, then we're going to Dave's where you'll probably want an encore."

Since she figured Mavis would score some table scraps at the restaurant, she didn't mix anything but hot water with her food. She remembered to give her a little doggie massage after she set the bowl down and Mavis didn't seem to have any complaints. Once she was done eating, Lizzy got her into her coat and harness and pulled her own coat out of the closet. "Ready?"

Mavis barked and wagged her tail.

Dave's was only three doors down from the Hummingbird, so it was a short walk. The noise level was the same as she remembered. Dottie waved at her from a rectangular table in the far corner. Her mouth moved as Lizzy approached but she couldn't hear her over the din. She was seated between Dennis and another man, who Lizzy guessed was her husband. He wore suspenders and had a long white beard. Suppressing a giggle, Lizzy noted some of Dottie's bright pink highlights had ended up on the tip.

Dennis stood and pulled out a chair. "It's been a while," he said, his mouth uncomfortably close to her ear. Lizzy took a step back and Mavis growled.

"Hey little buddy." Mavis barked at him as he squatted and held out his hand for her to sniff. "Does she bite?"

"I don't honestly know. She just showed up yesterday."

"Have a seat," Dottie hollered. "This is my husband Steve, and I guess you know Dennis."

"Nice to meet you. Have you ordered?"

Steve gave her a nod. "Just drinks."

As diners gradually finished their meals and either left or moved into the bar area, someone turned down the music and Lizzy relaxed in increments. For some reason she was finding Dennis annoying but couldn't figure out what had changed. He brushed his hand against hers, leaned into her when he spoke, and kept insisting she order a drink until she got irritated and shot a *help me* glance at Dottie the mind reader. With some kind of nonverbal signal, she alerted her husband who said, "Let's swap seats. Dottie wants to be able to chat."

Lizzy stood but Dennis grabbed her wrist. "I'm sorry. Please don't change seats."

Her eyebrows rose with her pulse as she attempted to pull away from him. Mavis growled. "Dottie invited me to dinner so I really should spend some time with her."

He let his hand drop and scowled at Steve.

When the waitress brought their food, she handed Dennis another drink. "This is from Stacy."

He looked toward the bar area and lifted his glass with a grin. "Thanks," he mouthed.

Stacy wiggled and fluffed her hair.

Trying to ignore them, Lizzy eyed her plate and said, "This must be enough for three people."

"Steve always helps me with mine, but you can take some home," Dottie said.

Mavis whined softly and Lizzy gave her a piece of chicken on a small plate.

The remainder of the meal passed pleasantly for Lizzy and when it was time to leave, Dottie asked, "Would you like me to walk you home? Steve can have another drink with Dennis and pick me up when he's ready to leave."

Dennis said, "I can walk her home since we're going in the same direction."

"I really wanted to see what you've done with the house," Dottie said.

Jason sauntered over to their table and smiled. "Good evening, Lizzy. I see you're out making friends. Good evening, everyone."

Giving him a smile in return, Lizzy said, "Good evening, Captain."

"I'm headed your way and wondered if you'd like a police escort." He winked.

"That's very kind of you. Thank you." *This is a side of him I haven't seen. I wonder what he's up to.*

Dennis clenched his fists and said, "There's no need. I live right across the street from her."

Steve threw his arm around Dennis' broad shoulders. "Dottie can go too, and I won't have to worry about her. We'll have that drink."

"Fine," he grumbled.

"You ladies ready to go?" Jason asked.

Lizzy stood and took a step toward him before pitching forward, her feet entangled in Mavis' leash. Jason caught her and helped her regain her balance, holding on just a moment longer than necessary. Then he squatted down and began untangling the leash. "Who is this naughty little canine? I didn't know you had a dog."

"According to Holly, she belonged to the people who used to live in my house. She moved in yesterday and made herself at home."

"Marvelous." He chuckled.

Once free from the leash, Lizzy got herself and Mavis bundled up, then picked up her *doggy bag* and said goodnight before following Jason and Dottie to the door.

The three walked in silence for a few minutes. Mavis barked at the wind and trotted happily next to Lizzy, her tail wagging. Lizzy enjoyed the soft reflection of the Christmas lights on the snow, wishing she could paint.

Finally, Jason said, "It looked like Dennis was giving you a hard time. I hope I didn't overstep, offering to walk you home."

"He was making me a little uncomfortable."

"I had Steve trade places with her," Dottie said.

"Text me if he gives you trouble." He handed Lizzy a card. "He's not a bad guy but he thinks he's a real Romeo."

"Thanks."

"Well, here's where I leave you. I'm headed over to Holly's."

Lizzy watched him cross the street, wondering if he was dating Holly. *None of my business.* She and Dottie crossed in the other direction toward her house. Opening the door for her guest, Lizzy turned on the light and gestured for Dottie to enter. She walked in and looked around. "It's magnificent," she said. "Holly told me you had completely remodeled it, but I wasn't expecting this. It's... it looks so much bigger. I bet it's nice and bright during the day."

"It is. The upstairs hasn't been done, but I only go up there to sleep anyway. Would you like some tea? Or wine?"

"No thank you. Steve will be here in a few minutes. I'm sorry about Dennis. He and Steve are friends, and I thought he had a girlfriend. He was dating that woman at the bar, Stacy; maybe he still is."

"He was coming on strong. If I were Stacy, I don't think I'd be very pleased."

Chapter 6

Nighttime Adventure

It was still early so Lizzy decided to write. She dressed as her main character and practiced belly dancing in front of her living room mirror. Mavis enjoyed their new game, running around in circles and biting at the veil. Thus inspired, Lizzy opened her laptop and began to type. Mavis burrowed into her bed for a much-deserved nap.

A knock on the door pulled her out of her story. Mavis ran barking and wagging her tail and Lizzy, glancing at the clock, saw it was two in the morning. *So much for my schedule.* She saved her work and shut her laptop. The person at the door knocked again. Lizzy stretched and went to see who it was. "Who is it?" she called.

"It's Holly. Sorry it's so late."

When she opened the door, Holly gaped at her.

"What?"

"Are those your pajamas?"

Lizzy looked down at her costume and laughed. "I was practicing belly dancing. Come on in."

"I saw your light on, so I thought I'd stop by and check on you. Here's your slipper, by the way. Jason said it was probably yours." She handed Lizzy the slipper she'd lost the night before.

"Thanks. One isn't much good."

"He also said Dennis was giving you a bad time."

"It was strange because up until now he's been a perfect gentleman."

"He hits on everyone. You have to be pretty clear when you say no, or he thinks you're playing hard to get."

"You've told him no?"

"He hasn't asked." Holly blushed bright red. "Why are you up?"

"I got home early and thought I'd work for a while. I didn't realize how late it was."

"I should go home and let you get some sleep then."

"Do you need some company?"

"I wouldn't mind. It's lonely wandering around in the middle of the night."

"Have you seen a doctor?"

"Yes, and I've tried all kinds of medication, hypnotherapy, ASMR, you name it. My therapist thinks it's because of childhood trauma but if you met my parents, you'd realize the likelihood is slim. I had a *Leave it to Beaver* family."

"If it was based on family trauma, I'd be the one with insomnia." Lizzy smiled. "Do you think a Malibu and orange juice might help?"

"Probably not, but I'll take one anyway."

The second Lizzy moved toward the kitchen; Mavis was on high alert. "Aueroo."

"Not yet Mavis. It's still too early. Do you want a treat?"

"Of course she does."

Lizzy took out a *Beggin Strip* and Mavis danced on her hind legs.

"Try closing your hand around the treat and knocking on the floor," Holly suggested.

When Lizzy did so, Mavis dropped and rolled over. "Cool! Good job Mavis." Lizzy gave her the treat. She got two glasses and some ice and poured their drinks, handing one to Holly and sitting with her at the table.

She was silent for a moment then said, "You know how you were asking me why I'm up in the middle of the night?"

Holly nodded.

"I don't really know if I've got a ghost or an intruder or what. I usually leave my things in specific places so I can find them. You know. Keys on the hook by the door. Laptop on my desk. You do that, right?"

"Sort of." Holly grinned.

"Well, I've been finding things moved around in the morning. One day I found my toothbrush in the refrigerator."

Holly raised her eyebrows.

"Someone broke in last night. That's why I borrowed your phone. But I can't figure out why that person would randomly move my stuff around. And if they are moving things, that means they're breaking in every day, not just last night. I wake up because I hear footsteps upstairs and I'm scared someone's in the house. I thought I was okay because I have a gun but after last night's break in and seeing that face in the window, I'm kind of freaked out."

"What face?"

"I think it was probably Mrs. Crocker. She's always peeping."

"What happened last night that was different?"

"Whoever was in the house turned out all the lights and the back door was open. I was terrified."

"I would've been too."

"I was wondering if you'd stay over. I'd feel safer having someone here with me."

"You want me to sleep here?"

"If you're not scared. I have six bedrooms on the second floor and a...I guess it's a third floor under the eaves but it's unfinished. That's where the footsteps are coming from."

"I'm in. I don't sleep anyway. If I'm here, you can get some sleep at least."

"Thank you!"

Lizzy remained at the kitchen table while Holly went home to get her pajamas and toothbrush. "Why did I ask her to stay?" she asked Mavis. "I don't want anyone to know who I am and I'm not even a good friend. I'm always wrapped up in my writing. She'll get tired of hanging out with me pretty soon."

"Who are you talking to?" Holly asked when she returned.

"Mavis." She laughed. "I spend a lot of time alone. Before she showed up, I just talked to myself."

"I've heard that's okay, as long as you don't answer."

"Uh oh. What happens if I answer?"

Holly tilted her head.

Rinsing their glasses and putting them in the dishwasher, Lizzy said, "I'm nearly dozing on my feet. Would you mind if I go to bed? You can watch TV if you want."

"I can try to sleep. Sometimes I can nap at strange times, even though I can't sleep at night."

"Come on up then. The second floor hasn't been redone, so it still looks like the 30s and the 70s had a baby." Lizzy led the way upstairs and into the room next to hers. "I'll be in there." She pointed. "And the bathroom is across the hall. If you hear anything, wake me up and we'll investigate."

"Okay. If I'm somehow sleeping, you wake me up."

"Deal."

She left Holly and brushed her teeth. Mavis was worried about missing something and wanted to sleep in the hall, but once Lizzy got into bed, she curled up next to her and they both fell asleep right away.

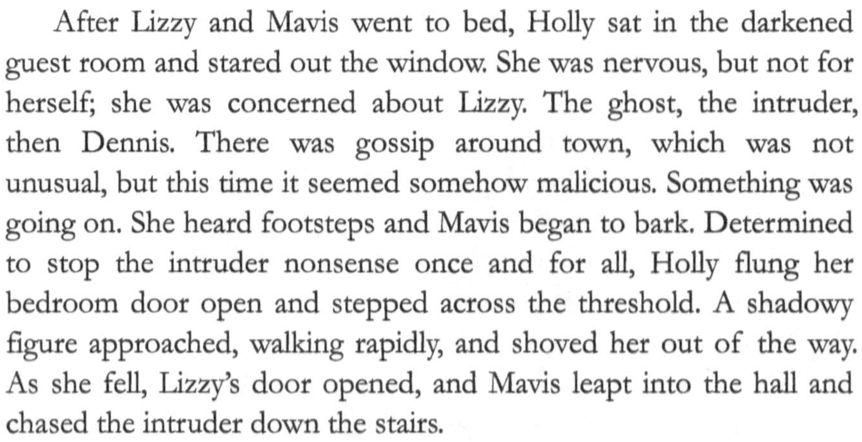

After Lizzy and Mavis went to bed, Holly sat in the darkened guest room and stared out the window. She was nervous, but not for herself; she was concerned about Lizzy. The ghost, the intruder, then Dennis. There was gossip around town, which was not unusual, but this time it seemed somehow malicious. Something was going on. She heard footsteps and Mavis began to bark. Determined to stop the intruder nonsense once and for all, Holly flung her bedroom door open and stepped across the threshold. A shadowy figure approached, walking rapidly, and shoved her out of the way. As she fell, Lizzy's door opened, and Mavis leapt into the hall and chased the intruder down the stairs.

Mavis gave a sharp cry. A door slammed. Holly rushed downstairs in time to see Mavis get up and race toward the door, running nose-first into the glass. She remained there barking until Lizzy appeared and switched on the light.

Rushing to the little dog, Holly picked her up and examined her. "Are you okay, puppy?"

Mavis struggled to get down and resumed barking as soon as her little legs felt firm ground.

"What happened?" Lizzy asked.

Holly told her and suggested they call the police.

"It'll be pointless. Whoever it was is gone now and since he knows I have company and we have a dog, maybe he'll think twice about coming back."

"He must be looking for something. The sooner we go through the stuff in the attic the better, don't you think?"

"I suppose. Saturday, right?"

Holly nodded. "I need to get my hair done on Saturday too. Would you like to come? We could take a break for dinner and go to the salon afterward."

"It probably wouldn't hurt. Can we go back to bed now?"

"Yeah. Goodnight, again." Holly slowly returned to the guestroom and examined her wrist. She hadn't mentioned it to Lizzy, but when the intruder shoved her, she tripped and landed on it. It wasn't broken, but she thought she might have a sprain. *I'll go see Doctor Steve tomorrow.* She lay down on the bed and watched the moonlight move across the ceiling. At some point she fell into a restless sleep, waking at dawn.

Impatient, Mavis barked sharply and nudged Lizzy with her nose. Lizzy rolled out of bed and went downstairs to let her out. She gave her some food and found Holly's note on the kitchen table.

'Had an early appointment. Made coffee. Thanks for the adventure. :)'

Smiling at her thoughtfulness, Lizzy glanced at the clock and told Mavis she'd be right back. She threw on her coat and rushed to the Hummingbird, intent on getting her morning pastry before Dottie sold out. When she pulled the bakery door open, the gaggle of women at the counter stopped talking and stared at her. Making their excuses all at once, they hurried out of the shop. Lizzy canted her head. "What's going on?"

Fidgeting nervously, Dottie said, "Ethel's been spreading rumors again."

"About me? What did she say?"

"She said you're a witch. She saw you floating around your house and chanting. She thinks you were casting a spell on someone."

"What an imagination."

Dottie wouldn't meet her eye.

"You don't believe her? Seriously?"

"Dennis fell and hurt his ankle last night," she mumbled.

"When was that? While you were at my house?"

Dottie finally looked at her.

"A spell would have been pointless *after* his accident. When would I have done it?"

"That's true."

"Do you believe in witchcraft?"

"I don't know. I never thought about it before. But even though Ethel is a terrible gossip, she doesn't usually make things up."

"She spies on me all the time. She probably saw me dressed up as a belly dancer and practicing the seven veils. And I do talk to myself, but lately I've been talking to Mavis instead."

Dottie shook her head. "I'm sorry. I don't know what I was thinking. Shall I try to straighten everyone out?"

"Nah. Let them think what they like. I'll practice my cackle."

"I don't know. It could get out of hand."

"It's okay. I don't mind. What happened to Dennis?"

"He was probably drunk and slipped on the ice. What can I get you this morning?"

"Do you have any more of those cranberry-orange scones?"

"I do. Fresh out of the oven."

"Great. Four of those please."

<hr>

On her way home, Lizzy pondered the issue of small-town gossip. It was easy to dismiss someone like Mrs. Crocker as a harmless busybody, but if her gossip hit close enough, the results could get ugly. Lizzy had seen it happen before. She thought about Mariah, an old friend whose marriage broke up when gossip about an affair turned out to be true.

As she unlocked her front door, Theo hobbled toward her waving. She waited for him while he slowed and stood catching his breath on her porch.

He took a final deep breath and said, "You're sure making a stir."

"Harperstown gossip flies fast."

He chuckled. "I wanted to ask you to dinner at my house tomorrow. I thought I'd return your hospitality and maybe get a game of cards out of you."

"I'd love that. Thank you. I have Backgammon and Cribbage if you like either of those."

"I do love a rousing game of Cribbage."

"Would you like to come in for coffee and a scone? I'm just returning from the Hummingbird."

"Won't say no to sweets." Theo rubbed his hands together and grinned.

"I have a sweet tooth too. Come on in." Mavis was barking frantically on the other side of the door as she unlocked it. "She's all bark and no bite," Lizzy said as she opened it. She was wrong. Mavis bared her teeth and growled, then she flung herself at Theo's boot and tried to nip his ankle.

"I'm sorry. I don't know what's come over her. I'll just put her in the other room."

She picked up the little dog and took her upstairs and into her bedroom. "I'm sorry Mavis, but I can't afford the legal costs. You take a little nap, and I'll let you out after he leaves." She felt bad, but Mavis had taken a dislike to her visitor, so she had to choose.

Back downstairs, she shared her coffee and scones with Theo, who repeated he was a retired teacher. *He looks like a teacher*, Lizzy thought, noting his button-down cardigan and neatly pressed slacks. His poof of grey hair made him look as if he had been caught in a brisk wind.

"I like gardening and cooking, but I miss my wife," he said. "Do you live by yourself?"

"More or less. Holly and Mavis seem to have moved in." She chuckled.

Glancing through the French doors at the untamed mass of vegetation, he said, "Perhaps I could help you with your gardening in the Spring."

"I might take you up on that. I've never had a garden."

"What do you do for a living?" he asked.

"I'm an accountant."

"That's a solid profession. I like what you've done with the house."

"It suits me better now."

He finished his coffee and stood. "I must leave, but thank you for your company, and the snack. I'll see you tomorrow at noon."

"I'm looking forward to it." Lizzy led him to the front door and said goodbye then went upstairs to check on Mavis. The silence was more troubling than the barking. She opened her bedroom door and stared in horror. The little dog was digging in the corner and had already pulled up two square feet of carpet.

"Mavis! Stop. What are you doing? Bad dog."

Pausing briefly to stare at her with big brown eyes, she went right back to digging.

Lizzy got on her knees and picked her up. "What are you doing, puppy? I'll let you out now; you don't have to dig."

Mavis whined and struggled to get free, but Lizzy carried her out of the room, closing the door firmly behind her. "Come on, let's get you a treat and play some fetch."

While she and Mavis played fetch in the front yard, she called Holly to tell her about the dog's odd behavior. "Do you think it had something to do with Theo's visit?" she asked.

"I'm not sure. Her reaction to him was strange but the two don't seem to be related. Did you check the floorboards around the area where she was digging? Maybe you have a mouse or something."

"Nooo. I don't want mice."

"I'll bring a crate over this evening so you can confine her if you need to."

"Thanks. Bring food too."

"I'll see what I can do." Holly was laughing when she disconnected.

Chapter 7

Hidden Treasure

During a previous fit of boredom, Holly had cooked several meals but two had ended up in the freezer. She eyed her casserole with distaste. *She's going to think all I can cook is ground beef. No, she won't care. She'll be glad I brought something.* Walking over to her bookshelf, she pulled out her favorite cookbook and placed it on the counter next to the large bowl. Then she went into the pet shop and picked out a roomy carrier. At five o'clock she flipped the sign on her door from open to closed and walked across the street.

Lizzy answered the door with Mavis squirming under her arm. "She wouldn't eat. She just stands outside my bedroom door whining and scratching."

"This should help." Holly held up the pet carrier. "Why don't we have supper then we can go examine the floor?"

"Okay. What did you bring?" Lizzy sniffed. "It smells delicious."

"It's a casserole I made last night. I brought you a cookbook too." Handing it to Lizzy, she carried the bowl into the kitchen. "It's my favorite. It has recipes for everything from pancakes to Chinese stir fry."

"I can't take your favorite cookbook."

"I'll get you one of your own, but I thought if I start showing you how to follow the recipes now, then when we get snowed in, you can feed yourself."

"I could just get some frozen dinners."

"What if we lose power and you can't use the microwave?"

"Now you're starting to scare me. How would I even cook?"

"We all have gas ranges, so even if the electricity is out, you can light it with a match."

51

Holly took some plates from the cupboard and set the table. "Let's eat."

Mavis, momentarily forgetting whatever she was looking for upstairs, sat staring intently at the table.

Lizzy dished a generous helping onto her plate. "I'm drooling again. What's in this?"

"Take a look at the bookmarked page."

Picking up the hardback three-ring cookbook with red and white checks on the front, she flipped through to Holly's bookmark. "Hamburger corn casserole?"

"That's it."

"Okay wait. I need to take a bite first." Lizzy took a bite, then another. "I love this." Fork in hand, she looked at the recipe. "The ingredients seem pretty basic: macaroni, ground beef, cream of chicken soup..." she continued reading, then took another bite. "You'll have to explain the directions though."

"That was the plan. Maybe tomorrow we can cook something together, after we organize the third floor and get our hair done."

"We're going to have a full day."

"Or we can eat some of the stuff I have in my freezer and cook on Sunday. Do you want to come to church with my family?"

"What kind of church?"

"Lutheran."

"I don't know. Let me think about it."

Holly didn't push. She helped Lizzy load the dishwasher before they headed upstairs to investigate Mavis' newest obsession. She took the carrier just in case.

As soon as Lizzy opened her bedroom door, Mavis ran to the corner, wagging her tail. "What have you found here?" Holly asked her, getting on her knees and running her hands along the wood.

Lizzy knelt too. Mavis pranced and whined.

"Here. Do you have fingernails?"

"Not really. I can't type if they get too long."

"How about a screwdriver? Or a thin knife?"

"I have a screwdriver somewhere. Just a second." She left the room and Holly had to hold Mavis, who was growing more impatient by the second.

When Lizzy returned with the screwdriver, Holly used it to pry a floorboard loose. Then she peered into the opening and saw a small package wrapped in newspaper. Reaching into the hollow space she said, "I hope it's not something dead."

She pulled the object out and Mavis tried to jump in. She got her head in, but her body got stuck. "What else is in there?" She removed the dog and used her flashlight app to see. There, pushed to the side, was a giant cobweb-covered rawhide bone. "It's bigger than you are." She reached her arm all the way in, up to her shoulder, and made a face as her fingers encountered the cobwebs. "You'd better love me forever, puppy." She extracted the bone and had difficulty holding Mavis back. "Just a sec. I need to rinse it off. Ugh. Gross." Mavis pranced behind her all the way to the bathroom, barking and wagging her tail. Once she had rinsed off the bone and patted it dry, Holly set it on the floor. Mavis walked around it, sniffing, then picked up one end with her teeth and drug it under Lizzy's bed.

"One mystery solved. What else did we find?"

Lizzy held up a small ornate box with rounded sides and a flat bottom, supported by four tiny metal feet. The hinge and the keyhole were also metal, the box itself decorated with dark blue velvet and gold filigree. She shook it and something inside clanked.

Picking up the newspaper it was wrapped in, Holly said, "This is from twenty years ago, but the bone hasn't been in there that long. Whoever hid it there must have moved it from some other hiding place."

"There's no key. Do you suppose this is what the intruder's looking for? Since he hasn't found it, we could put it back."

"Mavis kind of gave the show away." Holly nodded at the scratched floorboards and ripped carpet. "Do you have anywhere else you could hide it?"

"I could lock it in my safe."

Nodding, Holly said, "It's still early, so why don't we take a look upstairs? I'm guessing you haven't checked to see what kind of mess he made last time."

"I wish I could get someone to cart it all away and board up the entrance."

"Once we go through everything you can decide what to do with it. You could redecorate it like you did downstairs. I bet you'd love it."

"Yeah." Lizzy didn't sound convinced.

***

In fact, Lizzy was questioning her decision to move to Harperstown again. *It seemed like a cute, sleepy little town but maybe I'm not cut out for small town life.* She sighed and followed Holly to the third-floor staircase. Mavis wasn't as quick on the narrower, unfinished stairs so she picked her up and carried her to the top. Glancing at the stacks of boxes, she saw more had been disturbed.

"Look! Christmas decorations," Holly said. "We need to decorate your house."

"Do we have to?"

"Of course."

Mavis squirmed until Lizzy let her down, then trotted around the room, sniffing at the boxes. She sat in front of a medium-sized box and whined. Holly placed it on the floor and opened it, peeking inside.

"What's in that one?" Lizzy asked.

"Mostly clothes. Mavis really loved Helen." Holly's eyes got misty. She took out a few garments and examined them one at a time before refolding them and placing them on the floor. Mavis sat staring at the box and whined again so Holly felt around to see what else was in there. She pulled out a framed photograph and studied it.

"This is a picture of her." She handed it to Lizzy.

"Is that her husband?"

"No," Holly said after a pause. "I'm not sure who he is. It must have been a long time ago because she's very young."

Still feeling around in the box, she produced a rubber ball. Mavis barked and thumped her tail against the floor.

"Ohh *this* is what you wanted. How did you even know it was in there?" She rolled the ball across the room and Mavis went running after it.

Lizzy was still examining the photo. "He looks absolutely smitten with her, doesn't he?"

"Maybe she left a diary." Holly giggled.

Lizzy didn't smile. She suddenly needed to be alone. "Is it okay if we do this tomorrow? I'm really tired."

"Sure. I'm sorry. I know you haven't been getting much sleep." She bent to pick up Mavis, who growled and snapped up her ball. "Don't worry, I'm not going to steal it."

Following Lizzy back downstairs, she asked, "Are you okay?"

"Yes. I'll be better tomorrow."

After Holly left, Lizzy sat at her desk to write, but she lacked motivation. She looked up and locked eyes with Ethel Crocker. In her already bad mood, she strode to the door and yanked it open. Ethel was gone but she yelled, "Stop acting like a peeping Tom and mind your own business, Ethel Crocker." Mrs. Fickle's head slowly sank below the fence line.

Heading back inside, she decided to search for curtains on Amazon. She needed to measure her windows and didn't have a tape measure. Then she realized she had to have a way of hanging the curtains, a rod and rings perhaps. *I should just hire someone local to hang them.* She remembered seeing an interior design studio in Sioux Falls. *Who cares? I'm just going to move anyway, hopefully before I freeze to death.*

Opening her laptop, Lizzy found the place she left off and slowly forced the words onto the page. Somehow her mood flowed into her prose and her main character became moody and depressed. *Where's that coming from? That's not Rachael.* She deleted everything she had written and turned off the laptop, opting to read instead. She was in the kitchen making herself a drink when the doorbell rang. *Honestly. Does it never end?* She approached the door and called, "Who is it?"

"Dennis. I'm sorry to bother you, but could I borrow some butter? I'm all out and the grocery is closed."

Lizzy opened the door and led him back to the kitchen. "How much do you need? Will a stick do?"

"Yes. Thanks. I appreciate it."

"Butter is one of the few things I don't let myself run out of." She saw him to the door and got back to the task at hand. Armed with a substantial glass of Malibu and orange juice and her book, she lit a fire and sat in her lilac recliner with her feet up. Mavis squeezed in next to her and laid her head on her paws. Lizzy read for hours, until her eyelids grew heavy, and her book dropped from her hands.

Chapter 8

Body on the Floor

Knocking. Lizzy's eyes opened. Sunlight flooded the living room, and someone was knocking on the door. *Why isn't Mavis barking?* "Mavis?" Still lying next to her, Mavis didn't move, her breathing shallow. Lizzy rose stiffly from the recliner and hobbled to the door. Holly was standing on the porch. *It's Saturday.*

"I think something's wrong with Mavis. Can you take a look at her?"

"Of course." Holly looked past her, eyes widening. "Who's that?"

"Who?" Lizzy spun around and looked behind her. She didn't see anyone at first, but then saw the woman lying on the floor by her desk. She rushed toward her, groaning when she realized it was Ethel. She knelt by her side and took her pulse. "Call 911." Her voice shook. Remaining by Ethel's side for a few minutes, she grieved for a life cut short. She noticed the knife in her chest, surprised by the lack of blood. Then she realized she was kneeling in a puddle of water and started worrying she was messing up a crime scene. *It must be murder, right? She wouldn't have stabbed herself. Why is she in my house?* "Holly? Where are you?" Lizzy walked back to the front door and saw Holly on her cell phone outside, so she waited. When Holly disconnected, she repeated, "Can you check on Mavis?"

"Shouldn't you be more concerned about the body?"

"Didn't you call 911?"

"I did."

Holly was looking at her strangely. *What does that look mean? I don't have time for that right now.*

"Let's wait for Jason"

"Please. She's breathing funny. I don't want her to die."

"I'll take her to the clinic."

Relieved, Lizzy got Mavis' blanket from her bed and wrapped her gently, before handing her to Holly. Then she watched her carefully navigate the icy intersection to her clinic. The arrival of the police contingency distracted her momentarily. Captain Schneider and his dog, three additional officers, two paramedics, and Dottie's husband Steve arrived all at once.

"Where's Holly?" Jason asked.

"She took Mavis to her clinic. Something's wrong with her."

"Why did you kill Mrs. Crocker?"

"I didn't. Don't be crazy."

Jason just stared at her. "Let's have a seat in the kitchen and you can tell me what happened here."

"Can I make some coffee?"

"No. Sit down."

Lizzy sat. "Where do you want me to begin?"

"Begin with why she was here."

"I don't know."

"What time did she arrive?"

She shook her head. "Look, I was tired last night, and I couldn't concentrate on my work, so I decided to read. At some point I fell asleep. I have no idea what time it was, but Mavis hadn't asked me to go outside so it couldn't have been too late."

"Is there some purpose to this?"

"I woke to Holly knocking. Again, I don't know what time it was —whenever she came over. She said, 'Who's that?' and when I looked, I saw Mrs. Crocker lying on the floor."

"Were the glass doors open?"

"No."

"Were they locked?"

"I don't know. I took Mrs. Crocker's pulse, told Holly to call 911, and then went to find her because she didn't come inside." Lizzy cocked her head, wondering about that.

"Holly, whatever you might think, is not an idiot.

"She called me and I told her to go home."

"Why would I think she's an idiot?"

"She came over here and found you with a dead body on your floor."

"How would she know she was dead? I didn't even know until I checked her pulse. Is this how people in South Dakota show friendship? 'She's had three break ins and now someone's lying on the floor so she must be a murderess.'" Lizzy snorted. "Another master sleuth."

Jason was staring at her like she'd grown a third head. "You've had three break ins?"

"I just said that."

"Why have I only heard about one?"

"Because Mavis chased him off twice. And, that reminds me, why would I leave Mrs. Crocker in the middle of the floor? Wouldn't I take the body outside? I'm not an idiot either, Mr. know-it-all policeman. Only an idiot would leave a dead body lying where it can be seen from the front door. Maybe *you* killed her."

"Right. Because I don't like being a policeman."

"You're acting pretty suspicious."

"This is a pointless discussion. Perhaps I should take you in until you can give me a better explanation."

"Do whatever you want, but that's the only explanation I have."

"She's in your house and she was killed with your knife, from your kitchen."

"What's my motive?"

"You were yelling at her last night. What was that about?"

"She kept staring through my windows and when I opened the door to tell her to stop, she would run off. So last night I just yelled after her to stop acting like a peeping Tom. I don't think anyone has ever been killed for being nosy, but perhaps I'm wrong."

"I may be sorry, but I'm not going to arrest you right now. Don't leave town."

"I won't—yet. But I'm putting my house on the market and when this case is closed, I'm out of here."

Jason gazed at her. "Maybe you should stick around."

"Sure. It's the middle of winter, my new dog is going to die, and my only friend thinks I'm capable of murder. Good times."

"Do you have somewhere you can stay while your house is a crime scene?

"It just keeps getting better. I'll see if 'there's room at the Inn'."

"For what it's worth, I'm sorry. I know this is tough."

Lizzy shrugged. "Is it okay if I pack a bag?"

"Yes, and one of the officers can give you a ride."

"Not necessary." Holly was standing in the doorway. "You'll stay with me of course."

"The captain just got done telling me you think I killed Mrs. Crocker."

"Don't be silly. I know you wouldn't kill anyone. He's just being overprotective as usual." Holly glared at him.

"Overprotective?"

"You don't know. I keep forgetting you're new here. Jason's my brother."

Lizzy's brow furrowed and her fingers made her hair stand on end. "Schneider. I guess I should have picked up on that. You have a lot of nerve, Captain, putting words in your sister's mouth."

Holly put her hands on her hips. "What did you say?"

"All I said was you're not an idiot. Ms. Horn came to her own conclusions."

"Is Mavis okay?" Lizzy asked.

"She'll be fine. Someone gave her something to knock her out and they must have given her too much."

"So whoever killed Mrs. Crocker knew about Mavis."

"That doesn't help. Everyone knows everything around here, almost before it happens."

"Did they move her after she was killed?" Lizzy asked.

Jason stared at her.

"What I mean is, there's a puddle on the floor. Did they kill Mrs. Crocker in here, or did they kill her outside and bring her inside to frame me?"

<hr>

Refusing to answer Lizzy's questions, Jason sent a policewoman upstairs to keep an eye on them while they gathered her personal items. He watched them climb the stairs then sat on the sofa to think. Every ounce of his common sense told him four incidents in the same house were not a coincidence, but he knew in his gut Lizzy was not responsible.

Deputy Rice escorted Lizzy and Holly out of the house and perched on the coffee table across from him. She was the youngest member of his team and a strong proponent of following protocol. "Why haven't you arrested Ms. Horn?"

"She didn't do it."

"Then how did she know the body was moved?"

"It was a question, Rice. Give me a minute. I need to think."

She remained where she was, staring at him.

"Don't you have something you could be doing?"

She stood and frowned. "I don't like letting our prime suspect walk away from the crime scene."

"Do you think I would let her leave with my sister if I had any doubt?"

Rice shrugged. "Why don't you have doubts? That's what I want to know."

Tamping down his annoyance, Jason took a deep breath and refrained from rolling his eyes. "There are several reasons. We'll discuss them later. For now, I want to think this through, and I would like you to find something that needs to be done."

"Yes, Sir," she said stiffly.

Harvey looked up at him and whined. "It's okay, boy. I should have left you in the car."

He went back to contemplating Ethel Crocker's murder. Lizzy hadn't reacted at all to his comment about the knife and had shocked him with her final question. *She's sharp and perceptive. We could use more like her on the force.* Finally, he rose and approached Dr. Peele to ask his own questions.

Chapter 9

Houseguest

Lizzy had grabbed her most important possession, her laptop. She also took Mavis' bed and blanket and her giant bone, supposing the familiar items might comfort her. "I almost feel like I'm moving again," she told Holly as they crossed the street.

"I'm sorry all this is happening to you. I've lived here my entire life, except during college, and nothing ever happens."

Theo waved from his front porch. "Is dinner off?" he called.

Lizzy glanced at Holly, who shrugged.

"No, I'll be there. Can Holly come too?"

"Yes, that's fine." He waved again and went inside.

"I forgot my scones. Want to go to the Hummingbird?"

"Do you go there every day?"

"Not every day, but often."

Holly giggled. "Let's get your things put away and check on Mavis, then we can go."

Following her inside, Lizzy glanced around with interest. The age and architecture of their homes were similar, but the interiors were completely different. Christmas decorations and the style of the interior vied for her attention. "I don't even know what to focus on. Did you do all of this?"

"The previous owners put in the stone walls and giant fireplaces and something about it sparked my imagination."

"It's beautiful." Lizzy approached the staircase to inspect the intricate carving on the mahogany banister. "Like a cross between a medieval castle and a fairytale at Christmas. It'll take me days to explore."

Holly smiled. "I still add little touches here and there. That tapestry above the fireplace is new. Jason gave me the swords.

"He collects medieval weapons."

While plentiful, the Christmas decorations were understated. In keeping with the modern medieval décor, they were simple. Red bows, scented pinecones, candles. The show piece was an enormous pine tree. *It must be over ten feet tall.* Not gaudy like most trees she had seen, it was decorated with tiny white lights and candy canes.

"What's with the candy canes? They're all over town."

"It's a long story, but basically, a long time ago the people of Harperstown were hit with hard times. No one had any money to decorate for Christmas or to make special food, but one shop owner had made a mistake on an order and had hundreds of boxes of candy canes sitting in his storeroom. He donated them to the townsfolk, who put them to good use. We remember the shop owner and his selfless giving every year by decorating with candy canes and enjoying seasonal goodies like candy cane brownies and peppermint cocoa."

"Your brownies didn't have candy canes in them."

"I'm one of the few people around here that doesn't like them. Do you?"

"I don't know. I've never had one."

"But you've had peppermint, right?"

"That's a flavor of gum, isn't it?"

"Yes, but I don't mind the gum. You'll have to try a candy cane."

Lizzy's mind was beginning to wander. "What does your kitchen look like?"

"Leave your things by the stairs and come on through." Stone arches led from one room to another, and they passed through a dining room with a long wooden table and high-backed chairs into an enormous kitchen. The countertops and center island were topped with natural stone, Travertine Lizzy thought. The stove was placed inside a brick arch resembling a fireplace. A rustic-looking chandelier hung over the island. "I love my bright airy house but this…your house makes me want to write tales of knights and princesses."

She shook her head in amazement. "Stunning."

"Come on up and pick out a room. They're all different." Holly led Lizzy back to the stairs and helped her gather her belongings. She stopped on the landing and waited for her to look in each bedroom. More stone walls, tall narrow windows that arched and narrowed into points at the top. Enormous, canopied beds covered in sumptuous bedding. Some of the rooms had balconies and some fireplaces. They all had a simply decorated artificial tree in one corner.

"How can I possibly decide? Which one is yours?"

"Mine's on the third floor. You might like a room with a fireplace since it gets cold at night."

"Okay. This one." Lizzy placed her belongings on the floor and approached the bed, running her hand over the bedcover. The soft, blue silky fabric was patterned with navy and white brocade. A dark wooden table and upholstered chairs sat on a thick white carpet in front of the fireplace. "Is Mavis allowed up here? I would hate for her to cause any damage."

"These are just things. They aren't family heirlooms or anything. Come see my room and you'll understand what I meant about redecorating your attic."

Holly had taken out the wall, creating an open loft space and when Lizzy reached the landing, she involuntarily gasped. The room glowed. "It's a princess' room," she said. The floor was covered in shaggy white wall-to-wall carpet. Blonde wood framed the white walls and gleamed in the sunlight streaming through five windows with translucent white curtains. The sea of white was broken only by a red velvet bed cover with furry white trim and Lizzy thought it was the most beautiful room she had ever seen. She knelt and buried her hands in the deep carpet, reveling in the softness, then she flopped onto her back and rolled in it. "Like a teddy bear," she whispered. She got up and approached the bed to touch the velvet. "I want a room just like this one. Did you design it?"

"Yes. This is my happy place."

No one outside her immediate family had ever seen her room. Holly thought Lizzy might like it but didn't expect her to roll on the floor. Watching her with amusement she thought, *She's the antithesis of Heraclitus' quote. She'll surprise you whether you expect it or not.* "Are you ready to check on Mavis?"

"Maybe we should go get breakfast first. That way if she's awake we won't have to leave her right away."

"You have a point. Ready to go?"

Holly hadn't been to the Hummingbird for years, although she liked Dottie a lot. She enjoyed baking and certainly didn't need more sweets. She opened the glass door and feared the wonderful smells might bring her to her knees. *I should have eaten breakfast. This is dangerous.* She glanced at Lizzy, who was greeting Dottie with a smile. Then she noticed Dottie's guarded expression and glanced around. The other customers whispered amongst themselves, and pedestrians peered into the shop from outside. *This town.* She huffed. *Completely unable to mind their own business.* "Good morning, Dottie," she said brightly.

"Good morning, dear. Are you together?"

"We are. Lizzy's bunking with me for a few days while the police try to figure out what happened to Mrs. Crocker." *Might as well nip it in the bud.*

"What *did* happen to Ethel? I heard she was found in Lizzy's house," she said softly.

"Someone murdered her and took her into the house after they drugged poor Mavis. The police will figure it out."

"I don't know if I could live there after that," Dottie said.

"It's not the house, is it? It's a bad person. Once they're locked up the house will be fine." Lizzy sounded a little uncertain, but Holly hoped the other patrons would spread word of her innocence.

"Speaking of which, we should buy what we need and get back to check on Mavis."

Lizzy examined the delicacies in Dottie's glass cases. "How about…one of everything! Sorry. Just kidding. I don't know how to pick. Two chocolate croissants and a large coffee please."

"I'll have the same."

Dottie gave them each a small bag containing their croissants, leaning over the counter and whispering, "Can I come by after I close up? I have something I want to tell you."

Holly nodded and handed her a twenty, which she refused. "It's on the house," she said.

"Thank you, Dottie." Holly turned to Lizzy. "Put some cream in your coffee. I'm out at the moment."

"Thanks, Dottie," Lizzy said as she doctored her coffee.

Sitting together in the castle kitchen, Lizzy took a croissant out of the bag and examined it. The melted chocolate oozed as she took a bite, and she groaned with pleasure when it hit her tongue.

Holly watched her with a small smile. "You haven't said much about finding Mrs. Crocker. Do you want to talk about it?"

"So much happened so fast, I haven't really been able to process my feelings. I…it was so shocking seeing her there. I didn't really know her, and she didn't seem like a very nice person, but no one deserves to die like that." Lizzy pictured Mrs. Crocker lying on her floor, tears springing from her eyes. "Your brother said she was stabbed with one of my kitchen knives." She began to shake, belatedly, as she absorbed the reality of murder.

"It seemed odd how focused you were on Mavis, with Mrs. Crocker lying there."

"She was dead so I couldn't help her. They killed her right there while I was sleeping. How did I not wake up?"

The tears flowed unchecked, and she was momentarily unable to speak. "All I could think was Mavis might die too. I was so scared. I love her so much." She took a great gulp of air and shuddered. "I couldn't cope with both things at once. It was too much. And then your brother came and started saying the craziest stuff. Did you really think I killed her?"

Holly gazed at her. "That's how it looked at first and your reaction confused me. Jason told me to go home. But when I was looking after Mavis, I realized what you were going through and went back. Do you think it's possible you were drugged too? Did you feel fuzzy when you woke?"

"I did, a little. I thought maybe I had too much Malibu."

"Hold on a second. I'm going to text Jason. One thing's for sure; you're different, Lizzy Horn, but you're no murderer."

Chapter 10
Curious Events

The recovery bay where Mavis slept was in the clinic next to Holly's house. A covered breezeway connected the two so she could get back and forth quickly and in any type of weather. Still groggy but awake when they arrived, Mavis whined and thumped her tail weakly when she saw Lizzy.

"My poor baby." Lizzy reached into the crate and rubbed her ears. "Does she have to stay in here?"

"Maybe until after dinner then we'll see. She needs to regain her equilibrium."

"Can I hold her?"

"I don't see why not." Holly opened the crate and gently picked her up, handing her to Lizzy blanket and all.

Holding her like a baby, Lizzy rocked her back and forth until she fell asleep. "Will she stay asleep if we put her back in the crate?"

"Probably. She's still got whatever she was given in her system. I've sent a blood sample for testing, but it was some kind of sedative. She was lucky because whoever gave it to her wasn't worrying about dosage.

"That makes me so mad. They could have killed her."

Holly's pitying smile pulled her up short. "They did kill someone, didn't they. It still doesn't seem real." *This is stuff I write about but it's fiction. I've never even seen a dead body.*

"I haven't seen a dead person before, but I've had to deal with many dying animals. It never gets easier. Here, let me put Mavis in her crate and we can pop over to the hairdresser before dinner."

Lizzy gave Mavis a kiss and handed her to Holly. She was silent on the way to the salon, thinking about how attached she'd gotten to her little dog and wondering why she'd never had a pet.

The Cutting Edge, three doors down from Holly's clinic, had a plate glass storefront decorated with a simple rendition of scissors and the name written out in cursive handwriting. Holly opened the door, a little bell jangled, and eight women stopped talking and stared.

"Why lookee who's here. It's our town murderer," Stacey smiled wickedly and popped her gum.

Lizzy feigned surprise, swiveling her head. "Where?"

"Don't act dumb. Everyone knows."

"Well, can a murderess and her sidekick get their hair done today?" she asked.

"As long as I can post your picture on Insta when you get arrested."

"Sure. Why not? Have you decided on a clever caption?"

"How about 'She got my chair?'" Laughing manically, Stacy instructed her to sit. "What do you need done?"

"Just a trim and a touchup on my roots."

<hr>

Another hairdresser was taking care of Holly, who was watching Stacy with trepidation. *We should leave.* She tried to stand but Erin pushed her back down in her seat and put a cape around her neck. *This is not going to end well.* Erin turned her so she was facing away from Lizzy and began asking her about her cut. She worked slowly and kept her occupied, so she and Lizzy were both getting their hair washed at the same time. They returned to their seats with towels on their heads and when Stacy removed Lizzy's towel, the entire salon went silent.

"I hope you don't want me to pay for this," Lizzy said evenly.

"So you're a murderer *and* a welcher?"

"What I am is a person who has 500,000 followers on Instagram, and you've just committed hairdresser suicide. You're going to be famous."

Stacy swallowed and took a step back. "I can fix it."

"You really can't. You might be able to fix the color without frying my hair, but you can't make the chunks grow back. It'll be at least a month."

Holly was amazed at her composure. No one in the salon said a word.

"You won't really post this online, will you? It'll ruin me."

"What would you do if someone did this to you?"

"I…"

"You would ruin them," one of the other clients said. "You know you would."

Stacy started to cry. "It seemed like a good joke at the time. I didn't really think it through. Please let me try to fix it."

"I'm not sure if I'll bother posting about it but one thing I'm very sure of; you will never touch my hair again. I'll leave it like this for New Year's and go to Sioux Falls to get it fixed in January. Meanwhile, could I get someone to take a photo?"

No one moved.

"I'll take one when we get home," Holly said. "We have to get to Theo's for dinner. I'm sure he'll be impressed."

"Everyone in town is sure to admire this new style. They'll flock to Stacy so they can look just like me."

Stacy ran from the room and as soon as she was gone, all the customers began speaking at once. Holly stood and removed her cape. She walked the few steps to Lizzy's chair and reached out to touch her hair. "I'm so sorry. I should never have brought you here."

"Do you have a ball gown that will match?"

"Why are you being so calm about this? I would be in hysterics."

Lizzy shrugged. "It's short. It'll grow. But *man* is it ugly. Why don't you let her dry your hair and we can go?"

"I don't want to be here anymore. Let's just go now. I'll put on my hat."

Holly handed Erin her debit card, but she returned it.

"You don't owe anything. What Stacy did—it's not okay. I hope you'll come back."

Lizzy snorted. "Come back. That's a good one."

<hr>

The horrified look on Theo's face made Lizzy laugh.

"What happened and why are you laughing about it?"

"Oh Theo, sometimes you have to either laugh or cry. Can you believe a silly hairdresser did this to me on purpose because she's jealous?"

"Why silly?"

"Would you trust her with your hair after you saw this? Will anyone?"

"Absolutely not. What do you call that color anyway?"

"I don't know. It looks like swamp green to me. Too bad it's not Halloween."

"I admire your optimism, young lady." He patted her arm. "I'll be right back. I have to check on dinner."

He left them in the living room and Lizzy looked around. The sparsely furnished room held a comfortable leather sofa and recliner, a large television, and an artificial tree. "Isn't it interesting how all of these homes are a similar style but they're so different inside?"

Holly nodded. "Most of the owners made changes over the years. Do you want me to take your picture now?"

"Oh. That would be great. How about over here by the tree so the light's behind you?"

Holly took several from different angles and handed Lizzy her phone so she could check them. Lizzy turned to see them better and ran into a small end table, causing a photo to fall. Picking it up, she turned it over and stared at it. "Holly, look at this."

Holly studied it and handed it back. "It's the same one."

Theo returned from the kitchen and said, "What are you doing with that?"

He grabbed it out of her hands and put it face down on the table.

"I'm sorry. I accidentally knocked it over. Is that your wife?"

When he nodded, she said, "She was very beautiful. What was her name?"

"Janet." He cleared his throat. "Are you ready to eat?"

"Yes. It smells wonderful. What did you make?"

"Ribs and coleslaw. I hope you like it."

"Why would he lie?" Holly whispered on their way to the kitchen. Lizzy just shook her head. "Later," she mouthed.

Theo invited them to serve themselves from pans and bowls on the counter and they sat around the wooden table with plates piled high. "Did you make everything from scratch?" Lizzy asked as she gnawed on a rib.

"Yes, I did."

"I can hardly believe it. This tastes better than restaurant food."

"I agree. Everything is delicious." Holly buttered a home-made biscuit.

"What about the beans?"

"Those too." Theo chuckled. "I soaked dry beans then cooked them with bacon and collard greens, just like my mama taught me when I was a boy."

"I'm so impressed. Can you teach me how to make this?"

"Me too," Holly said. "I thought I could cook but you've taken it to a whole new level."

"I would be glad to. I don't use recipes; mostly I cook to my taste, and it doesn't always turn out the same. Would you like seconds or are you ready for dessert?"

"Dessert. Dessert! What is it?" Lizzy asked enthusiastically.

"Homemade peach cobbler."

"I think I've died and gone to heaven. Tell me you have ice cream to go with it."

He chuckled again. "I certainly do. That's homemade too. I have an electric ice cream maker, my one concession to modernity."

After dinner Lizzy offered to do the dishes, but Theo said, "I did most of them as I went. I'd rather play a game of cards over coffee."

"That sounds like a perfect end to our meal. Everything was delicious. Thank you so much."

Awake and alert, Mavis whined and pawed at the door of her crate when they returned. Holly let her out and she ran for the door. Lizzy counted when she assumed the position. "She must have really had to go. That's her longest one yet."

"You count?"

"Yeah. Sometimes they're really long, like this one."

"You're funny." Holly giggled.

Lizzy canted her head. Sometimes Holly had a strange sense of humor. "Are you feeling better puppy? Let's go inside. I have a surprise for you." They went inside the house and Lizzy said, "Hold onto her so she doesn't come up the stairs, okay?"

Picking Mavis up and scratching her ears, Holly waited for Lizzy to return with Mavis' bed and the giant raw hide bone. When she saw her things, Mavis wiggled herself free and as soon as her bed landed on the floor, she jumped in and burrowed into her blanket.

"I haven't worked at all today. Do you think I could work for a couple of hours, until Dottie gets here?"

"Sure. Maybe I can take a little nap."

Dottie woke all three of them when she rang the bell.

Mavis sounded the alarm as Lizzy rubbed the sleep from her eyes and Holly ambled toward the door. "Hi Dottie. Come on in." Lizzy figured she must be used to her guests' bemused expressions when they first saw her castle.

Dottie looked around with her mouth open. "Girl, this is straight out of a movie. Where are you hiding the knight?"

"Unfortunately, he hasn't shown up yet," Holly said.

"Hm. Unfortunately…fortunately…it just depends."

"Thanks for coming over. Can I get you anything?"

"What've you got?"

"Let's see. Coffee or tea, of course." Dottie stared at Lizzy with wide eyes as Holly walked over to a long narrow piece of wooden furniture and slid one of the panels open. "Then whiskey, rum, vodka, Sambuca, Amaretto, and wine."

"How about Sambuca over ice?" Dottie said mechanically, still staring at Lizzy.

"What's Sambuca?" Lizzy asked.

"It's a licorice flavored liqueur. Want to try it?"

Lizzy wrinkled her nose. "I think licorice is an acquired taste I haven't acquired yet. I'll have coffee."

Holly brought Dottie her drink and went to get coffee.

"What have you done to your hair, Lizzy?"

"Stacy thought she was being funny."

Swirling the ice around in her glass and watching the Sambuca cloud, Dottie shook her head. "Things are getting out of control. That's why I wanted to talk to the two of you. Steve was called to your house early this morning and from what he told me, I know you didn't kill Ethel. You're still officially a suspect though and I figured you'd want to clear your name."

"Why was Steve at my house?"

"He's the town doctor. We don't have a medical examiner so he's first at the scene."

Lizzy nodded and accepted the cup of coffee Holly handed her.

"Anyway, Ethel wasn't a very nice person."

"I met her."

"I don't mean just her personality. She had a mean streak and quite a few enemies, including Dave Moon." At Lizzy's questioning look she said, "Dave of Dave's Diner."

"What did she do to him?"

"They had an affair and when he broke it off, she told his wife, who promptly left him. Then she spread rumors about him all over town."

Lizzy raised her eyebrows.

"Like I said, not a very nice person. She argued with everyone and went out of her way to cause trouble." Dottie took a sip of her drink. "She lived on her late husband's pension, and I think she must have been running low because recently she began trying her hand at blackmail."

Holly opened her mouth to speak but Dottie held up a finger. "You want to know how I know, right?"

When Holly nodded, she said, "I know because she tried it on my husband. She told him she knew about a case where his negligence killed a patient, and she wanted three hundred dollars a week to keep quiet."

"What did he say?" Lizzie asked.

"He told her to do her worst. He's not negligent and he keeps careful notes about every patient and their condition. She didn't pursue it, but I've kept an eye on her and know of at least three other people she was blackmailing."

"Who?" Holly asked.

"The three I know of are Stacy, Coral, and Percy Fickle."

"Who's Coral?"

"She's a friend of Stacy's who works at the grocery store. You've probably seen her. She's always wearing crop tops and cowboy boots," Holly said.

"Yeah. I just didn't know her name."

"I don't know what she had on them, but I saw her collecting money from them."

Lizzy sat picking at her cuticles and squinting at nothing. "No shortage of motives."

When Dottie's phone buzzed, indicating Steve was waiting at the curb, she stood and said, "Thanks for the drink. You'll be at the party tonight, won't you?"

"We will. Thanks for the info." Holly linked arms with her, and Lizzy felt a little left out. Mavis walked out with her though.

She still seemed a little wobbly but when she saw Dennis standing by Steve's truck, she bared her teeth and growled.

He lifted his foot to kick her before he saw Lizzy scowling at him. "Why does your dog hate me so much?"

"Probably because you're the kind of person who would kick her."

Completely disregarding her comment he said, "Woah. What happened to your hair, babe?"

"Your girlfriend thought she was being funny."

"I don't have a—wait, do you mean Stacy? She's not my girlfriend."

"You might want to let her know."

He shrugged and turned back to Steve. Lizzy picked Mavis up and carried her back into Holly's house. *These people can be so rude.* She put Mavis in her bed and covered her up, then went back to her writing.

⚬⚬⚬

Holly watched Lizzy's interaction with Dennis out of the corner of her eye. When she returned to the house Holly thought she looked angry. Dottie's incessant chatter, having faded into background noise, stopped abruptly. She stared at Dennis with a frown. "Take me home now." Steve's ears were red as he put his truck into gear and pulled away from the curb.

"What did you say to her?"

"Mind your own business," Dennis growled.

"You're real popular today, aren't you?" Holly turned to go back inside.

"What do *you* know, Saint Holly?" Dennis called.

Turning back to face him she said, "I know you've managed to alienate four people in as many minutes."

"What four people?"

"Lizzy, Steve, Dottie, and me. That's four. Keep it up and you won't have a friend in town."

"All of you are being unreasonable."

"Sure. *We* are."

Lizzy looked up from her laptop when Holly slammed the door. "What happened?"

"I don't know what's the matter with Dennis. He's usually so charming but today he's acting like a big jerk."

"What did he do?" After Holly told her, Lizzy said, "We should go over everything we know so far and come up with a plan. Dennis' personality change is interesting. Could he have killed Ethel? Or maybe he suspects someone?"

Holly shrugged. "What would his motive be? Sure, she was grouchy and annoying but why kill her?"

"She was always spying on me and according to Dottie she was a collector of secrets. She might have witnessed something she shouldn't have."

"We can ask around at the party tonight. Do you want to see if one of my Christmas dresses will work?"

"Okay." Mavis' head popped out of her blanket when Lizzy stood. Staring at her intently, she said, "Arooerer."

"You must be starving."

Mavis danced around, wagging her tail. "Roherer."

"We should get her something to eat before we check out the dresses. I didn't bring her food."

"Don't worry. You're in the right place. I'll be right back." Holly went through the side door to her clinic and returned a few minutes later with a bag of food and a double bowl. "Come on into the kitchen." She kept walking, followed by Lizzy and Mavis, who was getting more vociferous by the second.

When Lizzy set the bowl on the floor, Mavis paused to see if she was going to get her doggie massage but then couldn't wait. "Poor thing," Lizzy said.

She tried to rub her ears, but she lowered her head and growled. "Alright then. I know you're hungry."

"I hope she doesn't throw it up. Inhaling food after a bout of poisoning isn't usually a good idea."

After she ate and went outside, she pranced upstairs with them to a spare bedroom on the second floor. Holly opened the closet and showed Lizzy a rack of dresses, some short and some long. "I've worn some of these but not all of them. This is the one I thought I would wear this year." She pulled out a red sequined gown.

"Try it on so I can see. It looks gorgeous." Going through the dresses one at a time she said, "These are all so elaborate. How about this one?"

Holly smiled at the knee-length blue chiffon dress Lizzy picked out. "Perfect. I haven't worn it so it's still new. Try yours on too."

They put on their dresses and admired each other in a floor length mirror. "Do you happen to have a wig?" Lizzy asked.

"I have a few. It's hard for me to wear them because I have so much hair." Digging through a dresser drawer, she pulled out a long, curly blonde wig. "Will this do?"

Chapter 11

Christmas Party

Dressed in their finery, accompanied by Mavis in her Santa costume, Jason picked Lizzy and Holly up and transported them to the Peele residence. He admired their dresses, and it occurred to Lizzy he hadn't seen her chunky toad-green hair. *If he doesn't think I'm a loon now he will after he sees that mess.*

The Peeles' house was outside of the downtown area and much more modern. An expansive lawn, littered with reindeer, plastic candy canes, and several enormous Bur Oak trees framed the path to a sprawling ranch-style home with the requisite sloped roof. Holly leaned toward Lizzy and whispered, "Dottie loves entertaining. Her back patio is going to blow you away."

Jason pressed the doorbell, which played Jingle Bells. "She does get into the spirit, doesn't she."

Dottie answered the door, dressed as Mrs. Claus. "Your outfit is very festive," Lizzy said, admiring her fur-trimmed dress.

"Thank you, dear. I see you've found camouflage for your new hairdo."

She touched her wig, and Jason raised his eyebrows in question. "I'll catch you up later."

"Come on through," Dottie said. "Everyone's on the patio."

Isn't it cold? How can they stand it out there? She shivered involuntarily.

They passed through huge rooms that screamed Christmas. Nearly invisible, the sparse chrome and glass furniture was overwhelmed by candles, garlands, lights, and an enormous tree. The spacious kitchen, also decorated with seasonal tea towels and candles would do a restaurant proud.

When Dottie opened the sliding glass doors to her mammoth patio, music and cheerful voices greeted them. Tall freestanding space heaters were strategically placed to provide warmth. Dozens of well-heeled partygoers danced or chatted at the round tables interspersed with decorated trees along the perimeter.

"Help yourselves to hors d'oeuvres and drinks. You don't have to keep sweet Mavis on a leash; she's a good doggy. Aren't you, girl? I have hostess duties, but I'll be back to chat." Dottie twirled in a circle before gliding to a nearby table.

"Would you like something to drink?" Jason asked.

"I'll have a Long Island iced tea if they have them," Lizzie said.

"Are those good? Maybe I'll try one too."

Jason asked, "Are you sure? They're pretty strong."

"I think I can manage one." Holly grinned. "Listen. They're playing *Happy*. I haven't heard this in years. Let's dance." She grabbed Lizzy's hand and drug her out on the dance floor where she threw her arms in the air and twirled around. Lizzy, not much of a dancer, other than belly dancing and Zumba, held onto Mavis' leash and moved sedately, giving Holly a wide berth.

Jason returned and handed Lizzy her drink. "Why aren't you out there with Holly?"

"She's pretty enthusiastic."

"What happened to your hair?"

"You'll see."

Dennis, flinging Stacy around the dance floor, spun her into an elderly man in a tuxedo. The man wobbled and fell backwards into Mrs. Fickle. They grabbed at air before landing in a heap on the floor. Ignoring them both, Dennis continued dancing, but Stacy tried to pull away and help them up. He yanked her back and moved off with her.

Lizzy watched Mrs. Fickle help the elderly man to his feet and lead him to a nearby table, glad Mavis was on the leash. Mavis didn't like Dennis at all. Jason was watching too.

"Have you noticed Dennis has been acting strange lately?" she asked him.

"Yes. We're keeping an eye on him."

"You're just in time. I'm parched." Holly took her drink from Jason and gulped half of it down.

"You should probably be careful with that."

"Stop being such a big brother."

Sensing an impending argument, Lizzy passed the leash to Jason and excused herself to go to the restroom. It took her a few minutes to find it and when she did, Stacy was coming out. Glancing up and down the hall, she pulled Lizzy inside and locked the door. Before Lizzy could panic, she whispered, "I feel like I owe you, so I wanted to warn you Mr. Fickle and Coral are spreading rumors."

"Aren't people in this town always doing that?"

"Yes and no. Pay attention. Mr. Fickle has been telling people you've been buying books about poisons and serial killers and Coral chimed in saying you bought rat poison at the grocery. They're trying to make it look like you killed Mrs. Crocker."

"Was she poisoned?"

Stacy shook her head. "That's not the point. The point is people around town will believe whatever they want to believe, and they want to believe an outsider did it."

Lizzy considered that. "What's going on with Dennis?"

"I have no idea, but he's getting on my last nerve."

"Can I make a suggestion?"

"What?"

"You're a beautiful woman and you don't have to be naked to get attention. You want men to admire you for your mind and personality too, don't you?"

"I'm not naked."

"You're not leaving much to the imagination."

"What do you know? Don't think we're friends just because I warned you. I just wanted to make up for what I did to your hair. You aren't going to post those pictures, are you?"

"I doubt it. I'm not really that vindictive but I won't be back to your salon. By the way, I heard Mrs. Crocker was a blackmailer. You know anything about that?"

She caught the little gasp and the clenching fists, then could almost see the wheels slowly turning in Stacy's head. "I thought she might have something on Coral, but it was so long ago," she said.

Lizzy gazed at her and waited.

"She used to be a rodeo queen and then she quit and went to work for her uncle. There were rumors. I think she might have been drugging the horses."

Oh Stacy. Throwing your friend under the bus again. "Did you and Coral have a disagreement?"

"No. Why?" The round eyes didn't fool Lizzy.

"First you told me she was gossiping about me, then you said Mrs. Crocker was blackmailing her. You're friends, right?"

Stacy blushed. "I think she's putting the moves on Dennis."

Someone knocked on the bathroom door. "I'll be out in a minute," Lizzy called. "I do actually need to use the restroom so maybe you can leave first."

"Yeah, okay."

"Thank you for the heads up. I appreciate it."

Stacey nodded and let herself out of the bathroom. Lizzy followed a couple of minutes later. She found Jason and Holly sitting at a table with Dottie and Steve. Jason pulled out a chair for her and asked if she was okay. "Yes, I was intercepted. I'll tell you about it later."

"Dottie was telling us Helen Pederson was Steve's aunt," Holly said.

"Yes. A delightful woman."

"Where's Mavis?" Lizzy scanned the patio.

"I let her off the leash," Jason said. "She's around here somewhere."

Lizzy frowned. "I don't think it's wise to let her loose after what happened last night."

"Sorry. I'll find her." Jason and Steve rose and left the table.

Lizzy watched them go, then addressed Dottie. "Do you think Steve would be interested in any of her things? I have an attic full of furniture, clothes, photos, you name it."

"I bet he would. He doesn't have much to remember her by, except a few old family photos. She died so suddenly."

"What happened?"

"She was having supper with her husband and a friend and had a heart attack or something. She died before they got her to the hospital. Fred was never the same. He moped around for six months and then just up and disappeared." Steve stopped by the table and invited her to dance, so she took his hand and waved.

The scenarios whirling through Lizzy's head came to an abrupt halt when she looked across the room and found Mrs. Fickle studying her intently. Christmas lights reflected off the red and green ribbons woven into her long braid. *I wonder what she's thinking. She's always popping up but doesn't seem to gossip like the others.*

Jason returned with Mavis, passed her leash to Holly, and held out his hand, bowing gallantly. His suit gave him a dashing air. "May I have this dance?"

Lizzy shivered slightly and nodded. *This is probably a bad idea.*

Leading her to the dance floor, he took her in his arms as *Always* by Bon Jovi began to play. He felt warm and comfortable pressed against her. *Dangerous.*

⁓⧯⁓

Holly watched them and smiled. *Maybe we'll end up sisters. Maybe I shouldn't have had that second drink. I need water.* She rose a little unsteadily and made her way to the bar. She picked Mavis up and pushed her way through the crowd, waiting patiently for the bartender to notice her. Smooshed between Percy Fickle and Dave Moon, Mavis growled at Dave, so Holly switched arms.

She remembered she wanted to ask Dave about his relationship with Ethel but got distracted by Mr. Fickle's conversation.

Although he was facing away from her, his voice was distinct. He always sounded like an erudite literature professor dressing down a less than astute undergraduate. Holly had been a victim of such a professor and did her best to ignore him. Unfortunately, she also liked to read. As the owner of the only bookstore in town, Percy was unavoidable. "You shouldn't be here," he told the man he was facing.

"Why not? I'm early, no one knows me here, and I could use a drink."

Holly noticed his shoulders and back stiffen.

"You'll ruin everything if you aren't careful."

"Worry about yourself and your blabbermouth wife."

"She's *your* cousin. We're doing fine."

"One more for the road and I'll meet you at eleven." The man waved at the bartender who walked past Holly to get him his drink.

She frowned and Dave said, "Don't worry. I'll get his attention on the way back. We're on a first name basis."

"Are you drowning your sorrows?"

"Sort of. Have you ever thought you hated someone and then something bad happened to them and you realized you didn't?"

It was a convoluted sentence, but Holly suspected he was talking about Ethel Crocker. She was saved from answering when Dave waved his arm and hollered, "Hey Van, over here. The lady wants a drink."

"What can I get you, Miss?"

"I'd just like a glass of water please."

"Water-schmahter. Get a real drink. I'm buying."

"Okay. I'll have a Long Island iced tea, but could I get the water too?"

"Yeah. How about you, Dave? One more?"

"One or three." He laughed.

"Do you know what time it is?" Holly asked.

"Not a clue." He picked up his tumbler and clinked it against Holly's. "Cheers."

"Cheers," she said, and chugged her water.

The song ended and Holly extricated herself from Dave, joining Jason and Lizzy at their table. Mavis was wriggling to get down. Holly placed her on the ground and passed her leash back to Lizzy thinking perhaps they should have left her at home. "Lizzy? I have to go to the restroom. Could you come with me and help with my dress?"

"Sure." She stood and handed the leash to Jason. "Be right back." She led the way to the bathroom, where they had to wait for a minute but once inside, she helped Holly with her long, fitted gown.

"I'm glad you came with me. I had no idea this dress would be so tricky, and those Long Islands hit me hard." She swayed slightly and hiccupped. "I asked you to come because I wanted to talk in private." She told Lizzy about Mr. Fickle's conversation then said, "We should figure out how to ditch Jason and follow him."

"Why don't we just ask him to go with us?"

"He'll either say it's not important or make us stay here and go himself."

"But we have Mavis too. Maybe we should ask him to take us home and then find Mr. Fickle."

"We'll have to follow him from here. I don't know where they're meeting."

Lizzy considered the problem. "What if we just wander off and he thinks we're still here. We can come back later and be like, 'Oh sorry. We were talking to so and so'. But how are we going to follow him? Do we take Jason's car too?"

"We could hide in his trunk?"

"In that dress? You'll never be able to climb into a trunk."

Lizzy thought for a moment. "Hold on. I have a better idea. Ask Jason to look after Mavis and ask to borrow his car. Tell him we have to run an errand. When he asks what, tell him it's a girl thing."

"What if he wants to come with us?"

"We can ad lib. Either tell him we'll be right back or let him take us to your house and make excuses. You have a car, right?"

"Yeah, but it's not very subtle. It's a bug with neon paint and peace signs."

"Figures." Lizzy rolled her eyes. "Hopefully he'll just let us use his car. It's already ten forty-five so we'd better get a move on."

Holly rearranged her skirt and washed her hands, then they returned to the table, where Jason was talking to Steve. He handed Holly his keys without question, so she and Lizzy were waiting in the parking lot when Percy Fickle left the party.

Chapter 12

Busted

Jason watched Holly and Lizzy enter the house. "What do you suppose they're up to?" he asked Steve.

"Do they have to be up to something?"

"Consider who we're talking about. We don't know Lizzy well, but I know Holly, and I suspect she's about to do something she shouldn't."

"Why did you give them your keys?"

"Don't worry. I have a tracking device on my car. I texted Barker to pick me up."

Steve chuckled. "Holly's a handful. Now she has an accomplice."

"I'm really glad she's found a friend, but I wish she would be more mindful of her safety."

"Do you think Lizzy's in danger? Ethel's murder was close. She was sleeping within view and if she woke up, we might have two murders on our hands."

"That's a frightening thought. I'd better head out. Barker's probably waiting for me."

"Take care. Hopefully I'll see you later."

Jason went out front just as Barker drove up to the house. "Where to, Captain?"

"Let's locate my car." Jason pulled up the tracking app, which was showing his vehicle moving slowly down Main Street. *What are they up to? Please let them be okay.*

⸺ ⋅⋅⋅ ⟨∽∾⟩ ⋅⋅⋅ ⸺

Lizzy and Holly had waited for Mr. Fickle to drive down the long lane to Boxwood Road and turn left before Lizzy put the car in gear and followed. The snow was falling again, large, lazy flakes innocently floating down to cover all signs of life. They discussed who should drive, since Holly was inebriated, and Lizzy had never driven in snow. Lizzy drove very slowly, with no idea where the road ended and the fields began. Using the streetlights as a guide, she hoped she wouldn't land them in a ditch.

Perhaps unsurprisingly, Mr. Fickle headed for his bookstore and drove around back.

"Park somewhere he won't notice the car," Holly said, so Lizzy parked in an alley on the opposite side of the street. Town Square Books was last in the row of shops at the end of the block, separated from the next row by a driveway for deliveries. Lizzy didn't see any lights inside, so she snuck to the driveway and peeked around the corner. Jerking back, she said, "There's a delivery van and several guys unloading boxes."

"I wonder what's in them."

"We need to get closer so we can hear what they're saying." She sprinted across the driveway to the bushes on the far side, then waited for Holly to join her.

"I'm scared. Maybe we should call Jason."

"Let's see what we can find out first," Lizzy whispered. She made it to the third bush before it snagged her skirt.

"What are we doing?"

"I'm stuck. Can you get me loose?"

The bush shook and the thorns seemed to multiply as they struggled to remove them from the delicate fabric.

A gunshot rang out, and a bullet hit the ground in front of the bush. "Who's there? Come out with your hands up."

They both put their hands in the air but only Holly stood. "My friend is caught on a bush. I was trying to get her untangled."

"Why are you in the bush?" he demanded.

"We were…"

The man misunderstood her pause for embarrassment and chuckled. "A couple of naughty girls, huh?" He tucked his gun in the back of his waistband. "Let me see if I can get her loose." He bent at the waist and fought with the bush for a few moments then when he said, "There!" Holly grabbed his gun and backed away. Lizzy watched in amazement as Holly shakily took aim and Jason sprinted up behind her, unholstering his own weapon. The man who had been helping her straightened and spun to face two guns. He gaped and put his hands in the air. "Who are you?"

"Harperstown Police. You're under arrest."

Holly turned slowly to face her brother's fiercest frown. "H-how did you know we were here?"

"We'll talk about that later. Go home. You can take my car."

"B-but what about—"

"Just do it. I've got backup."

Lizzy was struggling to get out of the bush so when Barker caught up with him, Jason said, "Get some ID and read this guy his rights, then we'll go see what's going on around back." He held out a hand and helped Lizzy disentangle herself.

"Thank you," she said quietly. "Where's Mavis?"

"She's in my car waiting for you. I'll be over to talk to you two when I'm done here."

"I'm sorry."

"We'll talk about it later. Go on home."

She nodded and went to catch up with Holly, surprised to find her trying to contain fits of laughter. "Talk about getting busted," she gasped. "You-you in the bush." She bent over laughing again.

Lizzy was puzzled by her mirth. "Doesn't it bother you that some guy shot at us and Jason's so mad?"

Sobering immediately, Holly said, "Oh. Goodness. This is how I deal with terror. I'll get over it."

"That was brave, grabbing his gun."

Tears rolled down Holly's face. "I wasn't thinking. I just didn't want him to kill you."

Lizzy stopped and hugged her. "It's okay now. Don't think about it anymore. How did Jason know we were here?"

"I think he has a tracking device on his car. It's lucky he doesn't trust us."

"I guess so, but I feel really bad about lying to him."

"He's used to it." Holly patted Lizzy's back and let go. "Let's go home and eat some brownies."

⁂

Reading the man's ID, Barker said, "Danny Carmichael, age 25."

"What are you doing in Harperstown, Danny?" Jason asked.

"Nothing."

"You shot a firearm within town limits."

"My friend is making a delivery, and I thought it might be a thief. It was just a warning shot."

"Have you had problems with thieves in Harperstown?" Jason raised his eyebrows.

"Nah. But you hear things, you know?"

"How many men are involved in this delivery?"

"Four including me and the shop owner."

"That would be Percy Fickle? Are they all armed?"

"I don't know, man."

"Take a guess," Jason said.

"Probably. They'll be missing me soon."

Nodding, Jason said, "Lock him in the cruiser."

"Aw, come on," Danny whined. "I didn't do nothing. I cooperated."

"We'll get it sorted out at the station." Leaving Danny in the cruiser, they crept around the side of the building. The half-unloaded van sat with the engine running and the back doors open but the delivery men were nowhere to be seen.

Nor was Mr. Fickle. The parking area had been plowed and footprints seemed to head in every direction. After searching the area, Jason said, "Call Nettle and Rice then take Danny to the station. We'll need to go over the van for prints and find out what kind of delivery merits armed drivers."

The sun was shining brightly by the time Jason arrived at Holly's. She invited him into the kitchen and offered him coffee. When he saw Lizzy, he chuckled.

"What?"

"Your hair. What happened?"

"Stacy got carried away."

He canted his head and studied her. "A skilled hairdresser could probably help."

"I know. I thought I would wait until after the new year."

Mavis sniffed at his ankles and wagged her tail when he sat at the table. She looked up at him with big brown eyes and whined.

"Sorry puppy; I don't have anything to give you."

Holly handed him a cup of coffee. "We could fix that. Are you hungry?"

Gazing at her, then at Lizzy with bleary eyes, he ignored her question. "Can you tell me why you decided to follow Mr. Fickle last night? I assume you followed him. That's why you borrowed my car?"

Lizzy stared into her cup while Holly explained.

"Dottie told us Mrs. Crocker was a blackmailer. She said she knew of three people she was blackmailing, and Mr. Fickle was one of them. Last night I overheard him talking to a stranger about a meeting at eleven so I told Lizzy we should find out what he was up to."

Jason studied Lizzy. "I expect this kind of behavior from Holly but I kind of hoped you would be more sensible.

"You were both in considerable danger."

"We didn't know," Holly said. "It's *Mr. Fickle*. We've known him our entire lives. What was he up to?"

"He's been receiving stolen goods and selling them online or in his shop. His contact in the organization is his wife's cousin."

"Was Mrs. Crocker blackmailing him?"

"I didn't ask for two reasons. The first is because you forgot to pass along that information and the second is because we couldn't find him." He frowned. "Who were the other two alleged victims?"

"Stacy and Coral," Holly said.

Lizzy told him about her conversation with Stacy and he shook his head. "That woman is something else. If you two get any more urges to investigate, could you run them by me first?"

Lizzy agreed. Holly opened the refrigerator door. "You guys want some eggs and bacon?"

"Holly."

"Yes, okay. We'll run our plans by you. Breakfast?"

"Thanks, but I'd like to get a few hours of shuteye. You don't need to see me out." He stood and headed for the door with Mavis at his heels.

⁂

Lizzy followed too and when they got to the door she said, "I'm really sorry about last night. I'd like to say it was all Holly's idea, but I got caught up in the scenario."

"I just don't want either of you to get hurt."

"I understand. By the way, do you happen to know when I might be able to go home?"

"You don't like Chez Holly?"

"No, it's marvelous and Holly is great company. I just like being in my own space."

"In a day or two, okay?"

"Thanks. I hope you can get some sleep."

They gazed at each other a moment before Jason said, "See you later." It sounded a little gruff to Lizzy, but she thought she knew how he felt.

"Bye," she whispered as he walked away.

She returned to the kitchen to find Holly whistling as she cooked a pan of bacon. Mavis sat at her feet, staring intently. "She's practicing ESP again," Lizzy said.

"She's good at it too. I already dropped two pieces."

Lizzy sniffed the air. "There's nothing like the smell of bacon."

"Tell me the truth. If I put a plate of bacon in front of you and a homemade brownie, which would you choose?"

"I can't have both?"

"Nope. Only one."

"Then I would pick the brownie, but I'd rather have both."

"I knew it." She giggled and placed a plate of bacon, scrambled eggs, and toast on the table. "Here's your breakfast. I think we ate all the brownies last night."

Lizzy poured herself another cup of coffee and sat down to eat. Holly joined her and said, "We should probably try to get some sleep. Why are you drinking coffee?"

"Habit, I guess. I always have coffee with breakfast. What did you do to these eggs? They're delicious."

"I accidentally discovered they taste great with dried horseradish, and I added shredded cheese of course."

"Horseradish? I wouldn't have ever thought of that." She took another bite and nodded.

After they ate, Lizzy helped with the dishes and fed Mavis, then they took her outside to do her business. As she was carefully sniffing for a good spot, Holly said, "What's going on over there?"

They watched as two cruisers pulled up in front of Lizzy's house and several police officers, including Jason, rushed inside. Mavis was finished before they exited with Dennis.

He was in handcuffs, but Lizzy couldn't see his expression from across the street. "Why was Dennis in my house? Did he kill Mrs. Crocker?"

"Oh my gosh. Why would he do that? Was she blackmailing him too?"

"What would she blackmail him about?"

"This is hearsay, but I heard the fire chief told his firefighters they'd be dismissed if they had anything to do with his daughter."

"What does that have to do with Dennis?"

"I'm always forgetting you're new in town. You don't know. Dennis is a firefighter, right? And Stacy is the chief's daughter."

"Ohhh. And the chief doesn't know they've been dating?"

"I can't imagine how he couldn't, but that might be why Dennis has been hanging out with you."

"Pft. That makes me feel special."

"You don't like him anyway."

"No. You're right. Not like that. I hope he wasn't the intruder because that would be creepy. If he was, though, what would he have been looking for?"

Shaking her head, Holly said, "I have no idea. Let's try to get some sleep and we'll grill Jason later."

"Sleep sounds good. Everything will make more sense when we've rested. Come on, Mavis. Let's take a nap."

Chapter 13

Why Kill his own Aunt?

The day that never ends. Just when he thought he could take a short nap, Jason's phone buzzed, and he was summoned back to Lizzy's house. Deputy Nettle reported a break in. After arresting Dennis Wright and transporting him to the station, Jason sat with him and asked why he had broken into the house.

Dennis didn't want to incriminate himself, but when faced with the evidence, his wallet in Ethel's pocket, he decided to tell his story. "Mrs. Crocker asked me to meet her at her house at eleven and she tried to blackmail me. She showed me pictures of Stacy and me and said she'd send them to the chief if I didn't pay her. I gave her three hundred dollars and told her it was a one-time deal; if she tried it again, I'd report her to the police. When I got home, I realized my wallet was missing but it was late, so I thought I'd go back and search for it in the morning." He sighed and his shoulders slumped. "The next morning everyone in town was talking about the murder and I realized I must have been one of the last people to see her alive. I needed my wallet back though. I walked around outside looking for it once I thought you guys had left. Then, after the party, I was drunk and got the bright idea of looking inside the house. I thought maybe she had picked it up and had it with her."

"What did she do with the pictures?"

"They were on her phone."

"What happened to her phone?"

"I think she put it in her pocket with the cash."

"Where exactly did you meet? Inside her house?"

"No, she was standing in her side yard and motioned me to follow her into the back."

"You were in her backyard. Was it dark?"

"Yes. It wasn't pitch black because of the moon, but pretty dark."

"Are you sure it was her?"

"Positive."

"She showed you the pictures, took your money, and then what?"

"I thought I put my wallet back in my pocket and left through the side yard."

"She didn't walk with you?"

"No, she stayed there."

"Do you have any theories about how she ended up dead?"

Dennis' brow furrowed. "No. All I know is she was alive when I left."

"Thank you. Barker will bring a statement for you to sign."

⸺•◦⸺⸺◦•⸺

A booming gong sounded, and Mavis' histrionic barking added to Lizzy's disorientation when she woke. She sat up in bed and looked at the clock. Twelve o'clock. Sunlight was streaming through the sheer curtains that hung from the glass wall of her bedroom. Getting up to investigate, she tripped over Mavis' giant bone on her way to the door, suddenly realizing Mavis was still on the bed, and still barking. "I'm going to have to get you some doggie steps," she said as she picked her up and placed her on the ground. She left her room and took the stairs to the first floor, where she found Holly at the door in her housecoat. *The gong must be the castle equivalent to a doorbell.*

Holly turned and smiled. "You're up."

"Who could sleep through that racket?"

"This is my mother. Mom, this is Lizzy."

They didn't look alike. Mrs. Schneider was tall and lean.

98

Jason had inherited her curly red hair and green eyes.

"You poor thing."

Lizzy was confused for a moment, until she realized Mrs. Schneider was looking at her hair, probably worse for sleeping on it.

"She was worried when Jason and I were absent from church and neither of us were answering our phones. I should have called but it didn't even occur to me today is Sunday. Do you want some coffee?"

"You said you were up all night. Don't you want to go back to bed?"

"I don't think I can. We slept about five hours, didn't we?"

"Something like that. I'm up for coffee."

"There you are, Mavis. I wondered what happened to you." Holly's mother bent down to rub her ears. "She was staying with us last winter, then she disappeared."

"I should have known." Holly giggled. "Now that you've met my mom, you'll know where I get my love of animals. We always had a stray or ten at our house when I was growing up. Plus, we lived on a farm; lots of chickens and cows."

Lizzy smiled, wondering what it would be like to live on a farm, or even to have a family that cared about each other. "I should go upstairs and get dressed. I'll be back."

<hr>

After Holly's mom took her leave, Lizzy asked, "Why didn't you tell her what's been going on? Wasn't she curious about why I'm here?"

"She knows about the murder. Everyone does. But you saw how worried she got when I wasn't at church. I didn't want to make her freak out. She invited us to dinner and the candlelight service on Christmas Eve, by the way."

Lizzy's stomach rumbled.

"I guess it's time to eat." Holly giggled. "I can make sandwiches. What kind do you want?"

"Anything is okay. I haven't met a sandwich I didn't like."

"Have you ever tried toasted tomato?"

"No…that sounds a little odd."

"I bet you'll love it."

Lizzy watched her make three sandwiches, toasting the bread and slicing two juicy red tomatoes. She buttered the toast and spread Miracle Whip on each piece before adding the tomato, salt, and pepper. Lizzy took a bite and groaned with pleasure. "Now I know why you made three. I want two."

"You can only have one and a half."

"Whyyyy?"

"Because I want two too. They're my favorite."

"It's amazing how something so simple can be so delicious."

The gong rang and Mavis, who was concentrating on the food, barked twice but didn't move. "I'll be right back. You two stay away from my sandwich," Holly said.

She went to answer the door and found Stacy on the porch, her eyes and nose red. Holly knew she was distraught because she was wearing sweatpants tucked into her boots. "Come in. What's going on?"

"I don't know what to do. They arrested Dennis and won't let me see him. They said he killed Mrs. Crocker. You're Jason's sister. You have to help me."

They walked into the kitchen together and Lizzy stood to get a cup of coffee for Stacy. "Did I hear you say she *has* to help you?"

"Augh. It's you again."

"What does she have to help you with, exactly?"

"To find out why Dennis was arrested and help clear him."

Holly saw Lizzy squint at Stacy and thought, *Uh-oh. Here we go.* But Lizzy didn't say anything. Mavis was barking and wagging her tail, even though Stacy gently pushed her away from her ankles with her toes.

"At least you could find out why they think he did it, right? Dennis wouldn't hurt a fly."

"What was Mrs. Crocker blackmailing you about?" Lizzy asked.

"She wasn't."

"If you want us to help, you need to be honest."

"I didn't ask *you* to help."

"We're a package deal," Holly said as she took a bite of her sandwich.

"That witch had power over me because she knew about something I did when I was a kid. If I tell you, I'll be giving you that power."

"We're not blackmailers, Stacy, and if you want us to help, we have to know certain things. How do we know you didn't kill her, or that Dennis wasn't trying to defend you? Do you know why he's been acting strangely since her death?" Lizzy was watching her intently.

When Stacy didn't answer, Holly asked, "Does your father know about your relationship?"

"Probably. Everyone else does."

"Do they really know? Dennis acts like he's a free agent, flirting with every woman in town. Has he ever mentioned he could lose his job if your father finds out about the two of you?"

"He asked me to keep it quiet, but he didn't say why."

"What if Mrs. Crocker had proof and threatened him?"

"I shouldn't have come." Stacy stood.

"We need to consider it from every angle. I'll see what I can find out from Jason," Holly said. "Stay and drink your coffee if you like."

"Thanks." She looked at Lizzy. "Your hair makes me cringe every time I see you. You should really let me try to fix it."

"No, thanks." Pausing and taking a sip of her coffee, she asked, "What else do you know about Mrs. Crocker? Did she have any close friends? Was she involved in any clubs?"

Stacy thought.

"It's funny how you can know someone most of your life and not really know them at all. She was like that. Dave Moon knew her well, I think."

"We could eat out tonight," Lizzy said.

"Or we could eat leftovers and ask Dave to meet us for drinks after supper. Otherwise, he might be too busy."

"I'll defer to your judgement. You know everyone much better than I do."

Stacy stood. "I should go. Thanks for helping me."

Holly walked her to the door and when she returned to the kitchen, Lizzy canted her head. "Are we helping her?"

"Inadvertently. What we're really trying to do is figure out who's been breaking into your house."

"Right." Lizzy shivered. "Because the only thing worse than an intruder is a murderous one. I can't even tell you how creepy it is thinking it might have been Dennis skulking around my house at night."

Mavis barked and ran toward the door and back again. "I think it's potty time. Why don't we take a little walk? Then I should try to get some work done. I can't believe how sidetracked I've been."

"I'll go visit Jason while you work. That way I'll be out of your hair."

"My hair." Lizzy snorted. "Sounds like a plan. Come on, Mavis. Let's take a walk."

<hr>

Theo stood on his front porch and waved as they passed. "Good afternoon, ladies. What's going on over at your place, Lizzy?"

"I don't really know. I'm waiting to hear when I can move back in."

"They arrested that young Romeo so perhaps it won't be long."

"Fingers crossed."

"By the way, I heard you offered Doctor Steve some of the Pederson's things. I was close friends with them and wonder if I might have a memento as well."

"I don't see why not. Maybe both of you can come over and take a look once I'm allowed to go home. Next weekend?"

"Thank you, dear. I appreciate it."

He went back inside, and they continued their walk, Lizzy observing the bourgeoning Christmas decorations with a critical eye.

They rounded the last corner and saw Jason leaning against his cruiser in front of Holly's house, Harvey at his side. Mavis saw them too and began barking and wagging her tail. As they approached, he smiled and waved.

Lizzy wasn't sure if she was happy to see him or not, but her heart did that little rat-a-tat-tat it did every time he was near, so she figured she probably was.

"I was going to drop by and see you," Holly said with a grin. "You saved me a trip."

"I wanted to talk to you both. Got any coffee?"

"Of course. If Lizzy didn't drink it all."

"We might need to make another pot. Mavis sure likes you."

"All the women do." Holly giggled and Jason blushed.

He bent down to pet Mavis, who rolled on her back and wiggled around. The pink had faded by the time he stood. When he bent over, Harvey got on his belly and crept toward Mavis. She scrambled to her feet and backed toward Lizzy, tail between her legs. Harvey whined.

"Keep an eye on him. He can be unpredictable," Jason said.

Holly led the way to the kitchen and went to check the coffee pot while Jason sat next to Lizzy at the table.

"The only thing missing is baked goods. I didn't get my Hummingbird fix this morning."

"I'll have to remember to bring some with me next time."

Lizzy's senses hummed at his close presence, and she fought the urge to move her chair either closer or further away. Apparently, Mavis felt the same way about Harvey, who lay on his belly again and kept trying to get closer. She approached cautiously to give him a sniff, then backed up again when he sniffed back.

Holly took them each a cup of coffee and sat across the table. "Tell us about Dennis."

"Mrs. Crocker had his ID in her pocket when she died and he broke into your house, presumably looking for it. I suspected the murder might have something to do with your intruder, so we've had an officer posted inside the house."

"So, you think he killed her?" Holly asked.

"Why would he kill his own aunt?"

Jason gaped at her. "His aunt?"

Lizzy covered her mouth. "I wasn't supposed to tell anyone."

"A bigger question is why didn't he mention it when I was interviewing him?" Jason took a sip of coffee and leaned back in his chair. He told them about his interview.

"And you believe him?"

"She had his wallet in one pocket and three hundred dollars in another, but her phone is missing. If he dropped his wallet and left, she might have picked it up. She couldn't have picked it up after she was dead. Plus, according to him she had her phone when she was talking to him. The doc said the time of death was between twelve and one so there may have been a second meeting, pre-arranged or not."

"You said she was killed with one of my knives," Lizzy said. "Was she killed inside the house?"

He paused before he continued. "This is confidential, okay?"

They both nodded.

"She was strangled outside, then taken into the house. She was stabbed after she was already dead."

"Why?" Lizzy asked.

"To set the scene, I guess. But an autopsy can show if a body has been moved and the cause of death."

"If the intruder is looking for something, he just caused himself all kinds of trouble. He wouldn't want the police staking out the house, would he? By moving the body inside, he's ensuring his search will be interrupted."

"First, we'll be clear that we don't know if our perpetrator is a man or a woman. Second, Ethel Crocker was a known busybody and a blackmailer. She might have seen something she shouldn't have and tried to blackmail the wrong person."

"I saw the intruder once," Holly said. "I'm lucky he didn't murder me."

Lizzy stared at her in horror and Jason sat up straight.

"Why didn't you tell me?" they asked in unison.

"It was dark so I couldn't see much more than his shadow. Plus, he gave me a shove as he went by and I fell, then Lizzy opened her door, and Mavis chased him down the stairs."

"Is that why you've been wearing that bandage on your wrist?" Lizzy asked.

Holly pulled at the stretchy wrap. "I sprained it when I fell. Doc Steve said to try to keep it immobile."

"What did he look like? It was a man?" Jason persisted.

"I don't know. It was so fast. He didn't look curvy like a woman but that could've just been a thick winter coat. He might be strong, or I might have just lost my balance because I wasn't expecting him to push me out of the way."

"Shoot. If you remember anything else, let me know."

"I will. I'm sorry I can't be more help. One thing we know is he or she doesn't like dogs. When Mavis chased him down the stairs, he kicked her and slammed the door and when he killed Mrs. Crocker, he drugged her. Mavis, that is."

"Mavis hates Dennis," Lizzy said.

Jason's eyes narrowed. "Something to keep in mind. I'd better get back to the station. I'll see you later." He looked down and said, "Good grief. What are you doing, Harve?"

They all laughed because Harvey was curled around Mavis, with her head resting on one of his enormous paws. Jason rubbed her ear. "I don't know how anyone could dislike this little cutie. Even Harvey loves her."

Chapter 14

What's up With Mavis?

Lizzy's mind was not entirely on her writing after Jason left. She kept thinking about his last comment, especially when Mavis started acting up. She dug in her bed, ripped up a paper Lizzy dropped, then grabbed her slipper and raced around the house with it. "Holly," she called up the stairs. "Mavis has lost her mind, and I need sugar. Want anything from the Hummingbird?"

"Yes. Let me put some shoes on. What's going on with Mavis?"

"I don't know." She told Holly about her antics and looked at her expectantly.

"Maybe she's upset about our strange schedule today. What time did you feed her?"

"It was earlier than usual. Six? But she talks to me when she's hungry."

"Ahroorohoh," Mavis said, as if on cue.

"Little scammer." Lizzy prepared her food and set it on the floor.

Mavis sat and looked at her, thumping her tail twice.

"Oh yeah. The doggie massage." She rubbed Mavis' head, neck and shoulders with both hands then straightened and turned to Holly. "Do you suppose we can leave her here to eat and take her out when we get back?"

"Maybe…can you be a good puppy until we get back?"

Mavis ignored her. She was busy eating.

"Let's give it a try. We'll be right back, Mavis."

When they got to the Hummingbird it was closed. "Nooo," Lizzy cried. "I need my sugar. Why is it closed?"

"We can try the grocery. They probably have something."

Slumping in mock defeat, Lizzy followed her down the street.

The grocery store was unusually busy. Small groups of shoppers clogged the aisles, gossiping about Dennis and the apparent crime wave in town.

"I heard the mob moved in."

"Ron said we should get a home security system."

"I bet Dennis is in the mob. I always thought he was hiding something."

"Stacy must be crushed."

"Let's get your sugar and get out of here," Holly said, tugging at her sleeve.

"Too late," Lizzy mumbled.

"Look. There's Lizzy. They found Ethel in her house."

"Hey, Lizzy. You found Ethel, right? Was there a lot of blood?"

"Holly, introduce us to your friend."

"How do we know she didn't do it?" Coral asked. Everyone stared at her in silence.

"Why didn't the police arrest you?" she persisted. "Is it because you're friends with Holly?"

"Sure," Lizzy said sarcastically. "Because that's the way the police work, ignoring evidence for friends and family." She rolled her eyes before grabbing two packages of cookies from the shelf and heading for the checkout counter.

Holly said, "Honestly, Coral, some people would call that slander."

They made their escape as the other customers went back to their conjectures with gusto. Holly was apologizing as she unlocked her front door, then froze. Mavis lay in her bed with her head under her blanket. Surrounding her bed and strewn around the entire living room were shredded papers from the coffee table where Lizzy had been working. "Oh my goodness," Holly said. "What is going on with you, Mavis?"

Walking over to the sofa, Lizzy sat with a heavy sigh. "I took notes by hand and I'm going to have to start over again."

"What were you working on?"

"I've been doing research on an unsolved robbery in Sioux Falls from twenty years ago. A man from Harperstown was charged and did time for the theft but the priceless coin collection he stole was never recovered. He claimed he was innocent, but all of the evidence pointed at him."

"Where is he now?"

"I don't know. He disappeared."

"Do you have a name? Or a picture?"

"His name was Carson Davies and the picture in the newspaper is ancient. It's not very clear. I don't think I can solve a twenty-year-old mystery or anything; I'm really just interested in the story because it was local." She looked at Mavis. "You've wasted a lot of my time, puppy."

Mavis pulled her head from underneath her blanket and whined. Then she jumped out of the bed and grabbed the corner of a newspaper she'd been laying on, dragging it to Lizzy's feet and sitting square in the middle. She moved aside when Lizzy bent to take the paper, staring at her with big brown eyes.

Reading the front-page story, which she had read before, Lizzy looked at Mavis. "Are you trying to tell me something?"

"Rroherer."

"I sound like a nut. Holly?"

Holly shrugged. "I've seen and heard of some unbelievable animal behavior over the years so I'm not going to say it's impossible. What's the article about?"

"It's about Carson Davies. He lived here in town and had an antiques shop. He was an expert in art, coins, and furniture."

"Why would Mavis have an interest in something that happened so long ago?"

"I don't know. Would Mr. Davies be around Mr. Fickle's age now?"

"Maybe, but—ohh, Mr. Fickle was arrested for accepting stolen goods."

"Hmm. You might have something there, Mavis. We should ask Jason if he can trace Mr. Davies' whereabouts."

Lizzy knew it was five o'clock when Mavis started dancing around on her hind legs and made a beeline for the kitchen, waiting under the arch. "Did you make an appointment with Dave?"

"I did. Seven o'clock. Why don't we join Mavis for supper, then we can get gussied up and go see him?"

"I can gussy all I want, and it won't help with this hair." Lizzy frowned. "I need to find some goth clothes, so it looks like I did it on purpose."

"I have a green and black pantsuit I bought online. It looks terrible on me, but I bet it would be perfect on you. I'll show you after supper."

"What are we having?"

"I made crockpot steak the other day and froze it. You won't believe how good it is. In fact, if we get you a crockpot you can make it. It's super easy."

Lizzy waited for Holly to heat up their dinner in the microwave, then put a little steak, potatoes, and carrots in with Mavis' dogfood, adding warm water to make it juicy. She set the bowl down and only massaged her ears for a second before she started wolfing down her meaty meal. By the time Lizzy and Holly sat at the table, Mavis was staring at Lizzy fixedly, as if she hadn't eaten in a week. "You're such a scam artist. I just fed you. Not only that, I fed you before we went to the store. You're going to look like a basketball instead of a football." She took a bite of steak, savoring the rich, beefy flavor. "Now I understand. This steak demands seconds."

"Delicious, right?"

"I definitely want to know how to make it."

"Have you ever used a crockpot?"

Lizzy stared at her. "I don't even know what that is."

"A slow cooker. You put the food in, set it on low, then at supper time it's ready to eat."

"That sounds like my type of meal. Except it requires thinking ahead."

"Don't worry. I'll help you make a two-week menu. Every day you can freeze half and pull something out when you don't want to cook."

"Which is every day." Lizzy laughed.

"But you like eating homemade food, right?"

"I like *your* food."

"It's all super simple, not like Theo's."

"That was incredible, wasn't it? I can't believe he made all that stuff. Even the coleslaw."

"Coleslaw isn't actually difficult, especially if you have an electric salad shooter."

"I'd rather just buy it at the deli. Can I have seconds? That's the best steak I've ever had."

"Sure. Help yourself." Holly bent and gave Mavis a little piece, almost losing a finger in the process. "Mavis likes it too."

"Of course she does. I think she might eat an old sock if it came from the table."

⁕⁕⁕

After supper, Holly took Lizzy upstairs to the *extra clothes* room. "With so many unused rooms, I figure I might as well spread out. My mom said I should open a bed and breakfast, but I like my privacy, and I don't have time. The clinic has been quiet this week but sometimes I get emergency calls in the middle of the night and on the weekend. It's worst during a full moon."

"I wouldn't want a bunch of strangers traipsing through my house either. In fact, I *have* had strangers, and I don't like it. At least one intruder, a dead body, the police…could it get any worse?"

"Don't say that! It can *always* get worse."

She chuckled but Holly was serious. "Don't invite trouble. You have enough as it is."

111

"Sorry. Where's that outfit you were talking about?"

Heading toward the closet, Holly slid open the door and began to sort through clothes that she either didn't like or couldn't wear. She had arranged them by color, so she easily found the outfit in question. Removing the hanger from the rod, she held it up for Lizzy to see. "It's a little small for me so I haven't worn it."

"Why didn't you return it?"

"I had this idea that I might lose weight and be able to fit in it someday."

"I used to do that too." Lizzy took the hangar and examined the stretchy dark green and black fabric. "You're right. This will go perfectly with my awful hair."

"Get dressed and I'll help you put on some heavy eye makeup and dark lipstick. You'll look amazing." She giggled and headed out the door. Looking back, she said, "I'll put on something dramatic too. We can make a bold statement together."

Unsure of what she had that could make a bold statement, Holly went upstairs to her room and looked in her closet. She found a pair of dark slacks and a red silk, wrap-around blouse. *This will work. With some bright red lipstick and red heels.* She got dressed and went downstairs to see how Lizzy was faring.

Lizzy was standing in front of a mirror, tugging at the stretchy material when Holly returned. "I don't know about this," she said. "It's so…sexy. Were you really going to wear this?" The stretchy shirt ended several inches above her waist, with sleeves that were snug at the top and flared at her wrists. The pants, also stretchy, hugged her hips and thighs before widening into bell bottoms. *I look very 70s vixen.* She smirked at herself in the mirror. "What will I wear on my feet?"

"Do you have any black shoes?"

"I do but they're at my house. I wonder if we can sneak in and get them."

"We can try. I don't think they'll arrest us for that."

"Your outfit is awesome. Those shoes make you look like a super model."

"Oh stop." Holly giggled and turned pink. "At least they make us about the same height, unless you're wearing heels too."

"I have some low-heeled ankle boots at home. I don't usually wear high heels. They make my feet hurt."

"Sit here and I'll do your makeup."

Lizzy sat and when Holly was finished, she looked at herself in the mirror. "What? I don't even look like the same person." Holly had applied dark plum eyeshadow, eyeliner, and heavy mascara along with dark plum lipstick; almost black but not quite. Lizzy studied herself from different angles then watched Holly make herself up. When she was done, Lizzy was impressed. Her dramatic, but lighter eye makeup and bright red lipstick went perfectly with her outfit. "Now you look like a pinup girl." Lizzy grinned.

Holly snickered and struck a pose that had them both giggling. "It's getting late, so let's see if we can get your shoes."

They crossed the street in snow boots, Holly's heels in her canvas bag. Lizzy tried knocking on the door first but there was no answer, so she used her key. Sticking her head through the doorway she called, "Hello?" Again, no answer. She walked in, followed by Holly and Mavis, and turned on the light.

"Good evening," Jason said. He had been sitting on the sofa in the dark but stood when the light went on, Harvey by his side. "To what do I owe the pleasure?"

"I did knock first," Lizzy said, wondering why she should apologize for entering her own house. "I need a pair of shoes."

His eyebrows rose. "That's an interesting look. What are you two up to?"

"We're meeting Dave Moon for drinks.

"I wanted to wear something that made my hair look like it was on purpose. Did I succeed?"

His slow grin gave her goosebumps. "Perhaps you did. You aren't supposed to be in here you know."

"Couldn't you escort us upstairs and make sure I only take my shoes? Otherwise, I'll have to wear my snow boots, and they'll completely ruin the overall effect."

"I suppose I can do that. Why are you meeting with Dave?"

Lizzy looked at Holly, who shrugged. "He just wants to meet Lizzy, I think."

"I always know when you're fibbing. Your ears turn pink. I think you're planning to ask him about Mrs. Crocker, right?"

Uh-oh. Busted again. Lizzy gulped.

"You're wasting your time, but I won't try to stop you. Just be careful and text me if anything goes wrong."

Chapter 15

Interview at the Diner

The diner was relatively quiet after supper on Sunday night. Holly led the way to the table in the corner of the bar where Dave waited. Mavis, forgetting her manners, barked at him. Feet firmly planted and tail tucked between her legs, her bark segued into a low growl.

"Good evening, ladies." Dave stood. "I see you brought Mavis."

"Yes, I hope you don't mind," Holly said.

"I don't, but she's never liked me. Perhaps she associates me with Ethel." He arranged his face into what almost passed for a smile. "I miss her, you know. Darn obstinate woman."

"I'm sorry for your loss. I'm Lizzy, by the way."

"I've heard about you and your unique hairdo." His smile that time was genuine. "I like how you've dressed it up."

Lizzy laughed. "Does it look like I did it on purpose?"

"I don't claim to be an authority on women's fashion, but I'd say you're rocking it. Please. Have a seat, both of you. What can I get you to drink?"

"I'll have a Long Island iced tea."

"Me too," Holly said.

Dave raised his arm, and a server scuttled over. "Two Long Islands and another for me, Bob. And a sampler platter."

"Yes, Sir."

"Have you tried the sampler?"

"All I've had so far are a sandwich and fried chicken. Both were excellent."

"And you don't come here often, do you?" he asked Holly.

"No, I usually eat at home."

The server returned with their drinks and a platter of assorted appetizers. Although she and Holly had just eaten, Lizzy's mouth watered at the sight of buffalo wings, quesadilla triangles, mozzarella sticks, stuffed potato skins, meatballs, and a pile of tater tots. "Does your chef use special recipes, or do you let him do his own thing?"

"We've worked on the menu together over the years. I don't know what I'll do when he retires. Sell maybe. Try some of these." He picked up a wing and took a bite.

Lizzy took a wing, and Holly took a mozzarella stick. Mavis whined so Lizzy surreptitiously passed her a tater tot.

"You said you wanted to talk to me about Ethel. What do you want to know?"

"Dennis was arrested for her murder, which seems kind of unlikely, and Lizzy is staying with me because her house is a crime scene. We were trying to figure out who her friends were or if she belonged to any clubs. No one seems to know much about her. What was she like? The real Ethel."

Dave nursed his drink without comment. He set the glass down on a napkin and looked Holly in the eye. "She was a good friend once you got past her prickly exterior. She was thoughtful and affectionate. We could sit for hours reading or doing a puzzle and didn't need to say much."

"Did she have any other friends?"

He shook his head. "I don't think so. She was friends with Helen before she died and a little friendly with Sage Fickle. She had trust issues. That's why she got so upset with me. She trusted me and I let her down." He finished his drink and signaled Bob for another. "I'll never forgive myself."

"Who do you think might have killed her?" Lizzy asked softly.

"I've been thinking about that." Bob brought his drink. "Would either of you like another?"

"I'll have one," Lizzy said.

Bob nodded and left.

"She could be vindictive if she thought she'd been wronged," Dave continued. "She told my wife about us and spread a bunch of rumors. I was…I was irate. She might have made someone else angry too."

"You haven't heard rumors about anyone in particular?"

"That's the thing. Ethel was a master at starting rumors that couldn't be traced back to her. A little whisper in someone's ear and before long the whole town was repeating it as fact."

Lizzy accepted her second drink from Bob and thought about Dave's words. One of her characters had been like Ethel. *I wonder if I should ask him about the blackmail. Does he know?*

She didn't have to bring it up because Holly did. "Did you know she was blackmailing several people in town?"

Lizzy cringed internally but Dave didn't appear surprised. "I've heard rumors. If she was, it started after we broke up."

"Have you heard any names?" Lizzy asked.

"No. Most people who are being blackmailed want to keep it a secret." He picked up a piece of quesadilla.

"True." Lizzy nodded and took another wing, deciding to change the subject. "I love these. I wish I could cook."

"That's why I'm here; so you don't have to." He grinned.

Mavis had settled down, opting to focus on food, so Lizzy gave her a meatball.

"If you don't have any more questions, I should get back to work. Please stay and enjoy yourselves."

"Thanks for helping us out, and for the hospitality."

"You're welcome, dear. It's always good to see you. Nice to meet you, Lizzy."

They ate and watched him silently as he stopped to speak with several customers on his way back to the kitchen. "How well do you know him?" Lizzy asked.

"You know what Stacy said about knowing Mrs. Crocker her whole life but not knowing her at all?"

Lizzy nodded.

"When she said that I realized I'm guilty of assuming I know people better than I do. Theo, for example. I thought he was just a cranky old man. He kept to himself and yelled at dog walkers to get off his lawn. But then he showed up at your door with flowers and he's been perfectly charming. I didn't even know he was a retired schoolteacher." Holly paused and stuck a meatball in her mouth. "Dave's a fixture in this town. I've known him since I was a child. If you'd asked me a week ago, I would have said I know him well, but I don't." She shook her head. "I know my clients well, and people from church…my parents' friends who've had supper with us, people I went to school with. Others, like Dave and Theo, I only know from brief interactions and their behavior toward others, and sometimes gossip. I would never have imagined Dave and Ethel sitting in her kitchen putting together a puzzle."

Fascinating. I wish I'd recorded that. I need to write it down. Essentially a monologue, Holly's answer to her simple question was more than she needed to know but as the premise for a novel, golden. "Are you ready to go?"

Holly narrowed her eyes. "What are you thinking?"

"I was just thinking about what you said. Are you about ready to go?"

"Yeah."

"Ready Mavis?" Lizzy checked the leash to make sure it wasn't wrapped around her ankles again.

The rest of the evening was uneventful. Lizzy sat at her laptop making notes and surreptitiously shopping for Christmas gifts on Amazon. Holly surprised her with a plate of sliced fruit breads. "Where'd these come from?"

"I was at loose ends. We have banana, cranberry, and cinnamon raisin."

"You just made them?"

"I did." Holly grinned. "Would you like butter?"

"You know me so well. Let's eat them in the kitchen and we can give Mavis a treat before we take her outside. I can't believe it's midnight already."

⁂

Still seated in Lizzy's darkened living room, Jason stared out her front window at Holly's house. He was relieved to see them return safely and wondered what they were up to as he watched the house for hours with nothing to do but wait. Stakeouts were usually mind-numbing exercises in futility but if Dennis wasn't the murderer, someone else might make an entrance once they thought the police had gone. Harvey alternated laying by Jason's feet and prowling the first floor, occasionally catching Mavis' scent and whining softly. His beast of a dog's fascination with the miniature dachshund bemused him. "You just never know where your heart's going to take you, do you Harve?" He pictured Holly wandering her darkened halls, wondering fancifully if people in the Middle Ages would have thought her a vampire. As he thought about Holly, it occurred to him that they hadn't really searched the upper floors of Lizzy's house. *The intruder was looking for something. I should look too, instead of just sitting here.*

Beginning downstairs, Jason used a penlight, making sure it couldn't be seen through the windows. Lizzy didn't have a lot of knick knacks or dust collectors, except for her books, neatly arranged on shelves in the open area next to her desk. One book was out of place, laying on the corner of her desk. Picking it up, he turned it over and stared at the back photo in shock. It was Holly. Then he looked more carefully and realized it wasn't. The author's name was Elizabeth Hornwhistle, and the lady on the cover was Lizzy. Although her brown hair flowed down to her waist, and she was twenty pounds heavier, he recognized her eyes that slanted up slightly and her full lips. *What else has she lied about?*

Moving upstairs to her bedroom, he discovered the flashlights and taser in her sock drawer and the floor safe in her closet.

I wonder what she keeps in there. Then he saw the damage Mavis had done to the carpet and got on his knees, where he found the loose floorboard. *Did she find whatever the intruder was looking for? Is it in the safe?* He overcame the urge to run across the street and ask when he discovered an old photo album. Pictures of Lizzy in her teens and twenties showed her enjoying time with a small group of friends. Although she did bear a striking resemblance to Holly, she was distinguished by a unique personality that shone through the camera lens. He could see it in her eyes, her impish smile, her choice of clothing. *Why did she leave her friends and everything she knew? Is there a warrant for her arrest?*

Replacing the album, he moved into the bathroom and found a phone at the bottom of the clothes hamper. The battery was dead, so he carried it into her room and plugged it in to charge it. He was so engrossed that he almost missed Harvey's sudden movement. His head went up and his ears flicked forward then back. "What is it boy?" Glancing at him briefly, Harvey was on his feet and out the door before Jason could react. He raced down the stairs to find Harvey barking and jumping against the French doors. *I might as well get some rest. He won't be back tonight.* He removed his shoes and lay down on the sofa, but sleep evaded him. Random thoughts whirled through his mind, twisting and turning, intersecting, and distorting until he drifted off.

"Sleeping on the job?" Barker asked sardonically.

Opening his eyes to find his sergeant's long nose two inches from his face, Jason said, "Back up, Barker." He sat and rubbed his eyes. "We had a visitor, but Harve chased him off. No sense staying awake when he wasn't going to come back."

"If you say so. Want some coffee?"

"Yeah. Thanks. What are we going to do about Dennis?"

"Rice released him last night, citing some rule about how long you can detain someone without charging them."

Jason slapped his forehead and spilled his coffee. "Ow! I was trying to eliminate him from our list of suspects. Now we can't be sure it wasn't him last night."

"I warned her."

Briefly closing his eyes, Jason sighed and pulled out his radio. "Rice, this is Captain Schneider. Please pick up Dennis Wright immediately and escort him to the station. Over."

"But, Sir…"

"Just do it. I'll be there in fifteen minutes."

"What's the plan?" Barker asked.

"I'll interview Dennis then set up an appointment for Lizzy Horn to meet me here. I have some additional questions. You keep an eye on things until I get back. We can't keep her away from home forever. I'll recommend the installation of a new lock and an alarm system."

The station was unusually quiet when Jason arrived. Rice looked up from her desk and cringed.

"Where is he?"

"I couldn't find him. He wasn't at his house or Stacy's, so I called the fire station, and the chief said he's taken a leave of absence. I'm sorry, Sir."

Her voice cracked and Jason hoped she wasn't going to cry. "Continue searching. Ask around and look for his car; it's a white 1969 Firebird Trans Am with blue stripes. Try to find out if he left town and radio me with updates."

"Yes, Sir."

He drove back to Lizzy's house. Harvey had his head out the window and whined when he saw Mavis. *Weird dog.*

He pulled up in front of the house and it occurred to him that he hadn't seen a garage. *Does she have a car?* He knew Holly did.

Harvey was struggling to get through the half open window. "Hold up, Harve. You're going to break it." He opened the passenger door, and Harvey took off before he could secure the leash, bounding through the snow toward Mavis. Lizzy grabbed the little dog and took several steps back. Recognizing the danger of such a move, Jason ran toward them, shouting, "Heel". He dove through the air as Harvey reached Lizzy, sitting in front of her and reaching his nose up to sniff Mavis. The last thing Jason saw were Lizzy's wide eyes as he grabbed at nothing and tucked himself into a ball as he hit the ground.

Groaning, he lay still for a moment, then opened his eyes to find Lizzy bending over him. "What was that? Are you okay?"

Holly was standing next to her shaking with laughter.

He groaned again. "I thought he was going to tackle you."

"He didn't want to hurt Mavis."

"Apparently."

"What did you want to see me about?"

"Give me a minute." Jason rolled onto his hands and knees with a grunt and stood. "Did you find something under the floor in your bedroom?"

"Yes. I totally forgot about that. Actually, Mavis found it. It's a fancy little box."

"Was there anything in it?"

"Yes, but it's locked."

"Could I take it if I give you a receipt?"

"Of course. It's not mine."

"Technically it is, since it was on the property you bought. What do you keep in your safe?"

"My gun, a few small valuables, and the box is in there."

"Could you show me?"

Lizzy led him upstairs and opened her safe. She sat back on her heels and stared. "It's empty."

Chapter 16

Moving Pieces

Finding Lizzy's safe empty was both disappointing and concerning. Not only was the box missing, but her unregistered gun had been stolen by a suspected murderer. Jason ran his fingers around the edges of his mouth, a habit he'd picked up when he suffered from chapped lips during the winter.

"Now what?" Lizzy asked.

"I need to think. Barker, escort them to Holly's house, get statements, and stay with them until you hear from me. Get a detailed description of every item in the safe." He turned to Holly. "The two of you stay put for now. We have two missing suspects and one of them has a gun."

"Who's the other suspect?" Holly asked.

"Mr. Fickle."

Lizzy's bottom lip quivered. She shuffled over to Mavis, who was curled up with Harvey, and said, "Let's go puppy." Mavis didn't budge and Harvey growled. "I might need some help with this."

"Just leave her here. I'll bring her back later," Jason said.

"I need her now."

Jason shrugged and approached the dogs. "Harvey, she has to go home now." When Harvey growled again, Jason took his chin in his hand and looked him in the eyes. "No. She's not yours." He picked Mavis up and handed her to Lizzy. "I'll be by later."

She didn't reply, and as she followed Barker and Holly out the door, he contemplated her unexpected responses to any given situation.

Lizzy told Barker everything she knew, then excused herself. She took Mavis and her laptop upstairs, leaving Holly to her own devices. Bored, Holly baked three different kinds of cookies. Barker sat patiently at the kitchen table and watched until Jason summoned him from Lizzy's house. Holly walked to the front door to see him out, then watched him cross the street. She saw him enter the house, then Jason left with Harvey. *I wish Lizzy would come downstairs. I'll take a walk then maybe she'll come down for supper.* She left the house, heading away from downtown. Catching sight of Dennis, walking up Mrs. Crocker's driveway and around the side of her house, Holly followed. "Dennis! Wait up," she called, trotting to catch up. When she rounded the corner, his arm shot out and encircled her waist, pulling her close. Then he did the unthinkable. He crushed her against him and kissed her until her legs were wobbly. She couldn't step back because his arm still held her in place, so she looked up—way up with round eyes.

"What are you doing here?" he whispered.

"I was just saying hello." Her voice sounded shaky to her own ears. Her whole body felt shaky.

"I suppose Lizzy told you Ethel was my aunt."

Holly nodded.

"I should have known she's like everyone else in this God-forsaken town. Did she tell you about my dad and everything?"

"No. She just asked why you would kill your own aunt. I think it was an accident."

"Well, you're here now so you might as well come in with me."

"What are you doing?"

"My aunt had a journal that she wouldn't want the police to get hold of. We're going to find it."

"I...I don't know if that's such a great idea."

"Do I have to kiss you again?"

"Have to?"

"Not that I didn't enjoy it, but it was the only way I could think of to keep you quiet. Come on." He held out his hand.

This must be how Cinderella felt, Holly thought, taking his hand and floating along with him as he broke into Mrs. Crocker's house.

Wishing he had taken that Time Management class the previous summer, Jason set his radio down and ran his finger around his lips. Too many things were happening all at once. He called Barker.

"I need you back here. They've found Mr. Fickle."

"I'll be right there."

Jason disconnected and sat on the sofa. He hadn't had a chance to ask Lizzy about that book, and the phone.

Barker tapped on the door and walked in. "Where'd they find him?"

"He was tied up in his storeroom the whole time. They've taken him to the station and Doc Steve is there with him now. I want to interview him before they take him to the hospital."

"No problem."

"How's everything across the street?"

"Holly's baking and Lizzy's been up in her room all afternoon."

"Stay sharp. Dennis is still missing and there's that stolen gun. Should I leave Harve here with you?"

Barker choked. "No, Sir. He can be scarier than a perp with a gun."

"You have a point. I'll be back as soon as I can. Come on, Harve. Time for a field trip."

Percy Fickle was lying on a cot in the medical bay with an IV in his arm. Steve looked up from the desk when Jason entered. The room, not often used, reminded Jason of the school nurse's office in elementary school and Steve could have been the janitor. He chuckled. *That beard.*

"How are you doing, Mr. Fickle?"

"I was so cold and hungry that I missed Sage's cooking. What took you guys so long?"

"We searched your shop on Saturday night, so we thought you'd scarpered."

"He pulled me into the closet and had a gun to my head."

"He who?"

"My wife's cousin, Gio. That creep. The next time I see him I'm going to deck him."

"Were you aware that you were receiving stolen goods?"

"They didn't say so, but I had my suspicions."

"Why did you do it?"

"Greed, I guess. I'm not usually a rule breaker but the shop hasn't been doing so well and the house needs repairs. I just thought I could make a little money on the side to help us get by."

"Did your wife know about it?"

"I don't think so, but you never know with her. She talks a bunch of mumbo jumbo about things that don't seem to mean anything. You know that saying *divide and conquer?* In her case it's *confuse and conquer.*"

Jason, who was acquainted with Sage Fickle, understood exactly what he was talking about.

"I've been a little worried about her. Is she doing okay?"

"I'll have someone check on her."

"What's going to happen to me?"

"I'm not sure. You might be able to get a reduced sentence if you're willing to testify against the guys who were delivering the goods. We'll have to talk to the District Attorney."

⁓

When Lizzy went upstairs, she locked herself in her room. *I should never have gotten up this morning. I came here so I could write in peace and now I feel like Faulkner. Maybe God doesn't want me to write this book. Will things keep getting worse until I give up?* She stretched out on top of her bed with Mavis and closed her eyes, trying to ignore the wetness leaking from the corners toward her ears.

She didn't want to get up; didn't want to leave her room, but Mavis was insistent. She barked and nudged and nipped until Lizzy sat up. Sighing, she trudged to the door and unlocked it. The house was silent, except for Mavis, who ran to the front door and barked. Glancing at a wall clock, Lizzy saw it was dinner time, so after she let Mavis out, she put some food and warm water in her bowl and gave her a little massage. The counter was covered with cookies. *Holly must have been bored.* She sat at the kitchen table and watched Mavis eat then got up and paced back and forth, pausing to look out the window.

Theo was in his backyard across the street. Wearing jeans and a hoodie, he was digging a hole, the muscles in his arms bulging as he bent to his task. She leaned forward, squinting. *Is that him? He looks fit and strong. His hair's the same.* Disappearing for a moment, he stood and began replacing the dirt. She shook her head. *I must be imagining things. It's pretty far but who else would be in his back yard? And that hair.*

Lizzy was on her way back upstairs when the gong doorbell sounded. *Where on earth is Holly?* She changed direction and answered the door, surprised to find Mrs. Fickle waiting on the porch. She greeted her and told her Holly wasn't home.

"That's okay dear. I really wanted to talk to you."

"Me?"

"May I come in?"

"Yes. Of course. Where are my manners? Would you like some coffee?" She backed away from the door so Mrs. Fickle could enter.

"No, thank you. I get overstimulated. Should I leave my boots outside?"

"Holly and I leave ours on the mat. May I take your coat?"

"No thank you, dear."

Offering her guest a seat in the living room, Lizzy sat across from her and asked, "What did you want to talk to me about?"

Mavis sniffed at Mrs. Fickle's sock feet and wagged her tail.

She gave her ears a little scratch and hesitated.

"Coming here seemed like a good idea but now I'm not so sure. You'll probably think I'm getting senile."

"Try me." Lizzy smiled.

"I always felt safe at home. Percy was there with me. Now he's gone and I'm afraid to go outside."

Lizzy canted her head. "But you walked over here."

"It's your back yard. I see people outside at all hours. So many. Sometimes I think I'm imagining things."

"People you know?"

"Mostly." She studied her hands. "It's like one of those mixed-up dreams you get when you eat too late at night."

"When did it start?"

"There've been ghosts since Helen died. I saw lights moving inside your house, but it got worse after you moved in. People keep trampling around in your back yard."

"Who've you seen?"

"Oh, let me see. I see Theo and Ethel a lot. You, of course. Then you found the body and the police were in and out. Doctor Steve was back there, and that nice young fireman. Sometimes I get mixed up. I thought I saw Holly one night and a lady wearing a big hat." She pursed her lips and wrinkled her nose.

"I can understand why that would make you nervous."

"Do you know why? Is there a reason why they're all in your backyard?"

"Some of them, like the police."

"Could I stay with you for a little while?"

She looked so forlorn. Lizzy didn't know what to say. "Why don't we wait for Holly to get home and ask her? My house is still a crime scene." *Where is she?* Lizzy didn't want company. She just wanted to shut herself in her room and mope.

Chapter 17

Family Secrets

It occurred to Holly that Dennis was pretty good at picking locks. She wanted to ask him if he was Lizzy's intruder but wasn't sure she wanted to hear the answer. He led her through the back door, into the kitchen and stopped. "If you had something you didn't want anyone to find, where would you hide it?"

"In a safe?"

"Besides being secretive, Aunt Ethel was cheap. I'm almost certain she wouldn't spend money on a safe."

"In the mysteries I read, sometimes the characters hide stuff in the freezer, or in containers with false bottoms."

"We'll start in here then."

"Could you kiss me again?"

Dennis approached her with a grin, and she blushed, realizing she had said it out loud. "Aren't you surprising," he said. "Just once. Then we need to find that book. We can save the fun and games for later."

That once kept Holly's brain busy for the entire search of the first floor. They searched for hollow books, under cushions, in every drawer and cupboard they could find. Then they went upstairs. Looking in drawers and under mattresses, Holly finally stopped and said, "Don't you think if you had something you used every day, that you might get kind of lazy about hiding it? I mean, it's inside her own house and even if she had company, she wouldn't expect them to rifle through her things upstairs. Would she?"

"So what are you thinking?"

"Where would she sit and write? Does she have an office? Or a desk at least? Is the third floor finished?"

"Let's look."

They found the desk on the third floor, facing a window that looked out over the neighborhood. The journal was in the narrow front drawer, along with several pens and a pair of readers. Dennis let out a whoop before shushing himself. Holly giggled. He sat on a nearby loveseat and opened the book, scanning a few pages. Inviting Holly to sit next to him, he slung his arm around her shoulders. "I need somewhere safe where I can read this. Can I stay at your house for a day or two?"

"Why are you hiding out? Didn't the police release you?"

"Rice released me, but then Jason told her to take me back in."

"How do you know that?"

Dennis' grin told her all she needed to know. *What a devil. Does he care about me at all?* "Lizzy's staying with me right now and Jason stops by all the time," she said.

His voice was seductive when he said, "You could hide me in your room."

"Why don't you just stay here?"

He frowned. "I guess I'll have to."

The pain was real. He was only charming her to get his way. Mavis would sniff him out immediately. She'd bark her head off and Lizzy would find out, then Jason would find out and think she betrayed him. "I can bring you some food and sit with you while you read."

"Food sounds good. I haven't eaten for a while."

Holly smiled. "I'll be back." She rose to leave, noticing that he didn't even glance up from the journal.

Checking to make sure no one was around before she left Mrs. Crocker's side yard, Holly crossed the street toward her own house. When she got there, she found Lizzy and Mrs. Fickle sitting in the living room.

"Hi Mrs. Fickle."

"Hello dear."

"Where've you been?" Lizzy asked, and she didn't know how to answer.

"I just took a walk. Have you eaten?"

"No. Have you?"

Holly shook her head. "I'll take something out of the freezer."

Lizzy got up and followed her to the kitchen, explaining why Mrs. Fickle was there and what she wanted.

"Would you be okay with that?"

"To be honest, I'm having a hard time with the constant interruptions, but how can we say no? She's old and scared."

"We could ask my mom. She likes company."

Lizzy's face brightened. "That's a great idea."

She wanted to tell Lizzy about Dennis but wasn't sure what her reaction would be, so she decided to wait. *Then again, he confided in her before, and she kept his secret. Maybe she would understand. Am I being naïve? We don't know who killed Mrs. Crocker or who stole Lizzy's gun. I should talk to her—after Mrs. Fickle leaves.*

Holly called her mother, who agreed to pick Mrs. Fickle up at her house, so she and Lizzy took Mavis and walked her home. The remaining snow on the sidewalks had partially thawed into slush. Lizzy wrinkled her nose. *Mavis is going to need another bath.*

Although well cared for, the Fickle house looked like it hadn't been updated in a hundred years. Lizzy prowled around the first floor while Holly followed Mrs. Fickle upstairs to help her pack. The first thing she noticed were the ample decorations. *I suppose when you've been decorating for decades you accumulate stuff.* Shifting her attention to the house itself, she admired the gleaming hard wood floors and the intricate wainscotting. *How does she manage the upkeep of such an enormous house?*

"My mom just texted she's outside," Holly said.

She carried a gigantic suitcase down the stairs, followed by Mrs. Fickle with an overnight bag. Lizzie couldn't tell how she felt from her expression, but she didn't seem as upset as before. "Is there anything I can do?" she asked.

"No, dear. Thank you so much for listening and for helping me find somewhere safe to stay. Thelma is a wonderful hostess. I'm looking forward to visiting with her."

Lizzy glanced at Holly, who said, "My mom."

Following them outside, Lizzy greeted Mrs. Schneider and put the luggage in the back of the minivan while Holly helped Mrs. Fickle get comfortable in the front. She was well into her story of recent events before the door was closed and didn't notice when the girls waved as they pulled out of the driveway.

"She seems to really like your mom."

"Everyone does." Holly smiled. "It's because she genuinely cares about them. Ready to go home?"

"Yeah." *Home. I've been staying with Holly longer than I lived in my own house.* "Do you suppose dinner is thawed?"

Mavis barked twice and Holly giggled. "You two are meant for each other."

Heading straight for the kitchen when they got home, Holly heated the defrosted pork chops and tomatoes while Lizzy set the table. She was nervous about really opening up but determined. When they sat to eat, she asked, "We're friends, right?"

"Of course." Lizzy took a bite and nodded. "This is really good. What is it?"

"Just pork chops simmered in canned tomatoes and Italian spices."

Lizzy put her fork down and gazed at her. "What is it?"

"Are we the kind of friends who can tell each other anything?"

"I guess so. We haven't known each other for very long but I don't judge."

"You don't have a crush on Dennis, do you?"

"No." Lizzy smiled. "Is that what's worrying you?"

"I've been in love with him for years and I've watched him hit on every woman in town, except me." Holly told her about their encounter that evening. "He made me feel so special. My brain shut off and I felt like it was a dream. He sat next to me with his arm around my shoulders, reading that book like we were a couple."

Lizzy sat silently, three little lines between her brows her only response.

"Then he asked if he could stay here. I didn't say no, but I discouraged him. He said I could hide him in my room, making it sound all sexy. But when I told him it wouldn't be a good idea, it was like I flipped a switch. He moved away from me and shut off the charm."

"He's trying to use you," Lizzy said gently.

"I sensed that. But I also felt like I would do anything to feel his affection again. I've waited so long for him to notice me."

"I know how you feel. I really do. But you need to be very careful. There's still a murderer running free, and someone has my gun."

"It couldn't be him."

"I'm not saying it is. Just be careful."

"I told him I'd take him food. Will you come with me?"

"Yes. That's probably a good idea."

"You won't tell Jason, will you?"

"Not unless you're in danger."

"What did he tell you about his family?"

"He asked me not to repeat it. Do you really want to know?"

She did but she didn't. "Please tell me."

So Lizzy told her about Dennis' parents and his reason for moving to Harperstown while she loaded the dishwasher and Holly packed a Tupperware container.

"Maybe we should leave Mavis here. She hates Dennis."

"True, but like you said, she's an excellent guard dog."

"Am I being stupid? Should I call Jason?"

Lizzy considered her question. "If you really love him, calling Jason will end it. If you have any doubts at all, we can just stay here. If you believe in him and his innocence, I'll go with you. It's your choice. You know him better than I do."

"Even if he doesn't care about me, even if he's using me, I don't believe he's a murderer."

"Then let's go take him some dinner."

They put Mavis in her soggy coat and harness and walked across the street. Holly hoped she wasn't making a fool of herself. *Even if I am, Lizzy will be there for me no matter what.*

The house was shrouded in darkness, and she was glad they brought Mavis. She knocked on the back door, which was locked.

Lizzy pulled out a key ring and tried several before unlocking the door. She chuckled at Holly's expression and waggled her eyebrows. "I have skills, baby."

"I won't ask."

"Probably better that way." They entered the kitchen, and Lizzy locked the door behind them. They wiped their feet on the door mat, but didn't remove their boots because the heat was off and the house cold.

"Dennis," Holly called. "Dennis?"

There was no reply, but Mavis flattened her ears and growled.

"Let her lead," Lizzy whispered.

"You said to bring you supper, and Mavis knows you're here. Just tell me if you want me to leave," Holly called.

Dennis' voice sounded low and dangerous when he answered from the darkness. "I also asked you to keep my whereabouts a secret.

"I saw the two of you from the window."

"I don't count. You already confided in me. I'm just trying to keep Holly safe. Maybe you should appreciate how much she believes in you and not try to drive a wedge between her and Jason. Do you ever think about anyone other than yourself?"

"Do *you*? I want both of you to leave now and don't bother telling the cops. I won't be here when you get back."

Holly felt the warm tracks of her tears as she turned and left the house. *He's not the man I thought he was.* She didn't stop outside to see if Lizzy was with her; she walked straight home and upstairs to her room. She wanted to be alone.

⸺⸺⸺ ⋅⋅⟨⊶⟩⋅⋅ ⸺⸺⸺

Lizzy wasn't behind her. She stayed where she was. "Holly left with your dinner," she said. "What are you trying to accomplish?"

Dennis stepped out of the shadows. "My dad's dead." His voice was flat. "He had cancer and told Aunt Ethel my mom kicked him out."

"I'm sorry. Is that why you wanted to find the journal?"

"Yeah. I was hoping to find out where he was. Now I don't have any reason to stay in Harperstown."

"Then why mess with Holly's emotions?"

Dennis gazed at her. "I really like Holly. She's the finest person I know, and she was the first person I met when I moved here. We started hanging out and Jason threatened to kill me if I touched her."

"You're afraid of Jason? Doesn't Holly get a say?"

"He's a cop and I thought my dad might be a criminal or something. He could have caused me a lot of problems. I kissed her today and I shouldn't have."

"Can I give you some unsolicited advice?"

"I wish you wouldn't."

"You have a nice life here: a house of your own, friends, a job you enjoy, and a woman who loves you. Go talk to Jason. Tell him what you've been up to. Tell him how you feel about Holly. Don't screw up your future by running away and leaving everything good in your life."

"Is that what you did?"

Her eyebrows rose. "What gives you that idea?"

"Just a hunch."

"Well, keep that hunch to yourself and think about what I said, okay?"

"Thanks. I haven't slept for two days, so I'll get some rest before I make any major decisions."

"Don't leave it too long."

Chapter 18

Caught in a Lie

Jason watched Lizzy and Mavis leave Ethel Crocker's side yard and cross the street. *What's she up to?* He knew better than to guess. She was always unpredictable. He left her house and met up with her in front of Holly's. *Does she look guilty?* "Where's Holly?"

"I'm not sure. Inside, I think."

"What were you doing at Mrs. Crocker's house?"

"Mavis decided to take a detour. I was just following her lead. No pun intended."

She's lying. "Let's find Holly. I have news."

Lizzy went upstairs, leaving him in the living room with Mavis, who pushed a pile of papers off the coffee table and started ripping them with her pointy little teeth.

"Naughty Mavis. What are you doing?" He took the papers from her and retrieved the others scattered on the floor. Glancing at the pages in his hands, he stilled and read over them more carefully. *Interesting. Why does she have this?* He sat mulling it over, jerking to attention when Lizzy returned with Holly. "Have you been crying?" he asked his sister. "What's wrong?"

"Nothing. I was reading a really sad book."

"Do either of you know where Mrs. Fickle is?"

"Yeah. She went to stay with Mom. She said she's been seeing all kinds of people in Lizzy's back yard and was nervous being home alone."

"We found Mr. Fickle and thought she'd like to see him."

"I'm sure she would."

"What did she mean about seeing people?"

"You should probably ask her directly. She named half the neighborhood."

"Yes. You're right. Where did this come from?" He picked up the pile of papers.

"I was doing some research. I lost a bunch when Mavis went on a paper chewing rampage," Lizzy said.

"Research for what?" Jason asked.

"It just seemed interesting. Local legend. I wonder what happened to Carson Davies."

"Or maybe you were researching for a book. Have you told Holly who you really are?"

Lizzy stiffened.

"What do you mean?" Holly asked.

Jason held out the book he found on Lizzy's desk. "Look at the back cover."

"Why did you really come to Harperstown? Was it because of that robbery you're researching? Or maybe because Holly looks so much like you?"

⁂

Suddenly understanding Dennis' fear, Lizzy felt like a rat cornered by a cat with razor-sharp claws. She didn't know where to begin, so she didn't say anything. Holly was crying.

"How can we believe anything you've said when you've been lying about even the most basic information, like your name. The cover says you're from Phoenix. It says you're engaged to a man named William. Where is he?"

Jason continued peppering her with questions. Holly wouldn't look at her. "I've read this book," she said. "There's a movie too. It's about a secret agent who betrays everyone for her job."

"That's not the point," Lizzy said.

"Then what is it? You said we were friends. I told you my secrets. And the whole time you were lying to me about everything. Was anything you said true?"

"Of course. Nothing has changed. I just worked really hard to escape my old life and don't want anyone to find me."

"Why did you have to escape? Did you kill someone?" Jason asked.

"How can you say that?"

"It's a valid question."

"No it's not."

Holly stood. "I can't be in the same room with you right now." She turned to leave and told Jason, "Find her somewhere else to stay."

"Thank you so much," Lizzy said sarcastically.

"Don't thank me yet. I'm going to have to arrest you."

"Because I gave a fake name?"

"No, because I found Mrs. Crocker's phone at the bottom of your hamper."

She thought he was speaking a foreign language. There was no way he was reading her Miranda Rights. But then he took out a pair of handcuffs and she knew it was true. "You can walk out to the cruiser on your own or I can cuff you."

"Do whatever you want. I don't care."

⁂

Jason's head and his heart were at war. He liked Lizzy and couldn't imagine her killing anyone, but her lies made him suspicious. He was confused by her actions and her attitude. But despite his personal feelings, Jason was first and foremost a policeman and the evidence was damaging. Leaving her at the station, he returned home and fed Harvey, then took him for a walk to clear his head.

He was in a foul mood the next day when Dennis Wright walked into his office and sat in the visitor's chair across from him. *Does no one knock?* "Why are you here?" he demanded.

"Haven't you been looking for me? Lizzy told me I should come talk to you. Have you really arrested her?"

Great. Now I have someone else questioning my actions. Like my own misgivings aren't enough. "I don't want to talk to you right now."

"You don't have to talk, but there are some things I need to tell you, starting with why I moved to Harperstown." He told Jason about his parents and his aunt. "I found her journal and read it, because I thought she knew where my dad is and just wouldn't tell me. I was right, in a way. She was a very spiteful woman. Anyway, here's the journal. It might help in some way. And there's one more thing."

Jason rubbed his eyes and glared at him, wishing he would go away.

"When I moved here, you warned me to stay away from Holly, and I have. But I love her, and I can't pretend anymore. If we can't have your blessing, I'll ask her to move away with me."

"If you've stayed away from her, how do you know she shares your feelings?"

"She's not subtle." Dennis grinned. "And that's one of the things I love about her. She's smart and loyal, and not a devious bone in her body."

"What about all your womanizing? If you hurt her..."

"I'm not going to hurt her. The womanizing, as you call it, was just me trying to distract myself."

"You might want to go see her then. She was devastated to discover Lizzy's been lying to her."

"How did she find out?"

"I confronted Lizzy while she was in the room. Did you know?"

"No, not really. I've just met people like her before and guessed she might be hiding from something or someone."

"You're not making me feel any better."

"Did you ask me to make you feel better? You said to help Holly out, and I will."

"Jerk."

"Yeah, I know. Just keep investigating. Lizzy didn't do it."

Mavis lay in her bed, watching Holly pace back and forth. If she stopped and looked at her, Mavis stared back with big brown eyes and whined. She wouldn't eat. Holly understood. She couldn't eat either. Instead, she baked. Her counters, table, and island were covered with cookies, pies, and cakes. When she ran out of space, she paced.

The doorbell rang, the gong sounding throughout the house. Mavis turned her head toward the door and barked, but didn't leave her bed. "Poor puppy." When she opened the door, Holly stood mute. Dennis waited on the doorstep holding a bouquet of red roses. It took her a moment to remember she was angry with him too. "Why are you here?"

"That seems to be the Schneider family motto today. May I come in?"

"I guess. Things can't get much worse," she said loudly, over the barking. Then she burst into tears.

Dennis wrapped his arms around her and hugged her while she cried. She knew it was an ugly cry, but it all came pouring out. She couldn't stop it. "I thought she was my friend," she sobbed. "Jason arrested her. Mavis is so sad. And you—you pretended you liked me so I would help you."

"Why don't we sit down, and I'll fill you in on some little secrets."

They sat on the sofa, and he put his arm around her, causing Mavis to go into guard-dog mode. She ran toward them, barking and growling. Dennis removed his arm and said, "Can you shut that dog up?"

"I'm sorry. She lives here and she doesn't like you. Maybe you should just put a little space between us?"

She thought he looked annoyed, but Mavis, although still barking, relaxed slightly when he slid away from her.

He raised his voice and told her about his family, why he'd come to Harperstown, his feelings for her, and his conversation with Jason.

"You love me?"

"I do."

"Why did you tell Lizzy about your family and not me?"

"That's the other one. I told her because I recognized her as a kindred soul. I knew she could keep a secret." She stayed last night and talked me out of running away.

Chapter 19

Stewing in Prison

Jail was not pleasant. Lizzy hadn't even gone to court or been arraigned but she felt like she might as well have been. Jason took her to the station and disappeared. She was left with strangers. A female police officer had taken her fingerprints, removed her personal items, and locked her in a holding cell. The cell had solid walls on three sides and was furnished with a lumpy cot and a toilet with no seat. The pounding in her head might have been from stress or the nauseating smell of disinfectant. At first, she was curious, observing everything from a writer's perspective and filing it away for future use. After the novelty wore away, however, she was stuck in a small space with nothing to do but think. She didn't want to think. Instead, she tried to sleep but the lights and the constant noise kept her awake. Then she tried exercise. She practiced her belly dance and did calisthenics.

The officers rotated bringing her food and water at mealtimes. Unlike the enormous prisons shown in movies, the small station didn't have a cafeteria or a cook. Her meals consisted of simple, relatively nutritious takeout from Dave's. She ate while balancing a tray on her knees. That was the highlight of her day, so she chewed slowly to make it last longer, mentally writing a description. She thought about the smell, the texture, what spices the food might contain. But the day stretched out before her and her mind began picking at her situation.

The first thing that crossed her mind was that no one came to visit. Her internal dialogue was contentious.

I thought I was making friends. Some friends.

You said you wanted to be alone and now you are. Isn't it better to be alone than to have a bunch of fake friends?

Being alone and being in jail are two different things. I wanted to be alone with my writing.

Isn't that just a prison of your own making?

Why was Holly so mad about me using a fake name? Who cares what my name is? How can Jason think I'm a murderess? I can't believe he arrested me. When am I going to get out of here? Will I ever get out of here?

Maybe they'll just let me rot in jail. They've probably forgotten all about me already. Once she allowed herself to start thinking, she couldn't stop. Her mind went round and round, her thoughts becoming ever darker.

When dinner was delivered, her thoughts shifted to Holly. She took a bite of pork chop and as she chewed, she thought, *Holly's were better than these. I miss her meals.* Then she realized that she missed more than Holly's meals. She missed Holly. Holly was a great friend. She was kind and loyal, always thinking of others. And she was fun. *I bet she could make jail fun.* She frowned to herself, remembering their conversation the night before. "We're friends, right?" Holly had asked. *What kind of friend am I? Am I any better than those friends I left behind? My lies hurt her because she felt like I didn't trust her. It wasn't about my name. She trusted me when she told me her secrets. I'm a terrible friend.*

She stared at her tray; her appetite gone. *I need to solve the murder so I can get out of here and make it up to her. How do I solve a murder the police can't solve? And how do I solve it from in here? Do I have enough clues?* Lizzy thought about Mavis. She missed her too. That sweet little dog had adopted her and loved her, imperfect as she was. She stuck to her side and snuggled with her when she slept. *I hope she's alright.* She pictured Mavis tearing up her papers and a tear rolled down her cheek.

⁕⸻⟨⟩⸻⁕

Holly was thinking too. After Dennis left and she tried to feed Mavis, she said, "Let's go for a walk, girl."

Mavis gave a weak thump of her tail and whined. "She'll be home soon. You can help me dig up some more clues." Someone knocked on the door and Mavis got into her bed and burrowed her head under her blanket.

Opening the door to her brother, Holly glanced back at the little dog. "She blames you."

"Who? Mavis?"

"Yeah. How's Lizzy?"

"I hear she sits staring at nothing and didn't eat supper tonight. We need to get her out of there."

"You put her in there. Can't you take her out?"

"It doesn't work like that. She's our only suspect and we have evidence. I can't just release her."

"Tell me about the evidence."

"Mrs. Crocker had her phone the night she died. She showed Dennis photos of him and Stacy when she tried to blackmail him. But when we found her body, the phone was gone. I found it in Lizzy's hamper. The battery was dead, so I didn't realize whose it was until later."

"I don't want to say anything against Dennis, but he's the only one who said she had her phone. And the disappearance of the phone might be evidence against him, if it didn't have those pictures on it for example, but why would Lizzy be worried about you finding it? What does it have to do with her?"

"Has Dennis talked to you?"

"Yes, he has and I'm very happy."

"Then why would you bring him up?"

"This isn't about Dennis. It's about Lizzy. She had no reason to hide that phone. Someone was trying to frame her."

"I thought you were mad at her."

"I am mad. No, I'm hurt. I feel betrayed. She was never really my friend, but that doesn't mean she's a killer."

Sitting on her cot, deep in thought, Lizzy was annoyed when an officer brought in a loud drunken man, pushing him into the cell next to hers and telling him to *sleep it off*. She couldn't see him, but he didn't sound familiar. At first, he yelled at the officer who brought him in, threatening him and kicking at the bars of his cell. Then he sang off key, making up verses when he apparently forgot the words. That might have made for an entertaining scene in one of her books. It was also disruptive, and she was trying to think. He finally passed out, but his snoring was almost as loud as his singing. *I wish I had some headphones.* She pushed the snoring to the back of her mind and concentrated on remembering everything that had happened in her house since she moved in. It was a lot, but she went over each incident, one step at a time. There was only one conclusion, and it sounded absurd, even to her.

Jason sat staring at his broken pen. He'd drummed it on the desktop until it snapped. Making up his mind, he pushed the button on his intercom. "Ask Barker to report to my office, then release Ms. Hornwhistle. Notify her that she can return to her home. It's no longer a crime scene."

"What should I write on the paperwork, Sir?"

"Lack of evidence."

Barker rapped on his door before entering and handed him the order for release to sign. "What's going on?" he asked.

"We don't have evidence to hold her but I'm sure she has something to do with all this so I'm going to tail her."

"Someone else could do that."

"No, I want to catch her red handed. Did you run a background check?"

"Yes." Barker hesitated.

"Well? What is it?"

"She doesn't have a record, not even a parking ticket. But when I inquired with the Phoenix PD, they sent me a long list of reports she filed, everything from assault to breaking and entering, all within the last year.

"Do they have an explanation for that?"

"Apparently, some of her fans and the paparazzi got really aggressive when her book was optioned. The police recommended she hire security and then she just vanished. The officer I spoke to sounded relieved to know she was alive and well."

"Did he sound like he knew her personally?"

"She, not he, and no. She just sounded concerned by her sudden disappearance after all those incidents."

"Let me know when she's released."

Lizzy was baffled. She had been released without any explanation and told she could go home. The first thing she did was head for Holly's house. She needed to set things straight and she needed Mavis. Shifting her weight from one foot to the other, she chewed on a fingernail as she stood at the front door and rang the bell.

She heard Mavis before Holly answered and gathered the little dog into her arms when the door opened. Mavis wiggled around and tried to lick her face. She looked at Holly and said, "I'm sorry. I was wrong not to tell you everything. You're the best friend I've ever had, and I didn't even consider how you'd feel about my fake persona. I was only thinking about myself. I'm terrible and selfish. I'm pond scum. Please forgive me."

Holly's face crumpled. "I'm sorry but I don't feel like I can trust you anymore. I'll get Mavis' things. She's missed you." She went inside and returned with Lizzy's laptop, the dog bed and the leash. "I've packed up your other belongings. I'll leave them on the porch, and you can come back for them." She stepped back and shut the door.

It hadn't occurred to Lizzy that Holly might not accept her apology. She stood immobile for a moment, blinking back the tears that threatened. Then she picked up her things and marched across the street.

Dennis met up with her as she approached. "Welcome home. I see you're a free woman."

"Not now, Dennis."

"What's wrong?"

"I'm just tired. We can talk later, okay?" Without waiting for an answer, she unlocked her door and went inside. Leaving her boots and coat in a jumble by the door, she set Mavis down and carried her laptop and the dog bed to her desk. Looking around, she felt no affection for her home. It was familiar yet alien. Her lip curled. "I hate you," she told the house.

Mavis looked up at her and whined.

"I guess it's just me and you, puppy. Are you hungry? Let's see what we have to eat." She had left Mavis' bowl and food when she went to stay with Holly, so she fed her first. She set the bowl on the floor and gave Mavis her doggy massage, but she didn't eat. Kneeling beside her, Lizzy said, "What's wrong? You're always hungry."

Mavis climbed onto her knees and pressed her head against her. Moving into a cross-legged position, she pulled Mavis close and held her. She kissed the top of her head and stroked her ears. "I'm sorry," Lizzy said. "I didn't leave you on purpose. I'm back now." *I don't need friends. Mavis loves me no matter what.* She hugged her again. They sat on the kitchen floor for a long time, until Lizzy said, "I'm hungry Mavis. Can we eat now?"

Mavis wagged her tail and licked Lizzy's hand.

"We'll have to get you some fresh food because yours looks all soggy and nasty." She got up and retrieved the bowl, dumping out the old food and replacing it. When she put it on the floor and gave Mavis a pet, the little dog was ready to eat.

Lizzy pulled out a frozen pizza and stuck it in the microwave. *Desperate times.* Mavis sat at her feet and stared at her as she ate. "This isn't very good, anyway." Taking a bite, she studied Mavis' intent gaze, her large intelligent eyes. "How do you keep digging up clues? Are you really that smart, or is it all coincidence?"

Mavis gave a sharp bark, her gaze unwavering.

"You can't possibly read. How would you know those papers were significant?" She shook her head and tore off a little piece of cheese, nearly losing a finger when Mavis grabbed it.

After Lizzy left Holly's, Jason knocked on her door. "Who is it?" Holly called.

"It's me. Can I come in?"

Her eyes were red and puffy when she opened the door.

"What happened?"

"Lizzy came over and apologized."

"Then why are you crying?"

"I told her to go home. Why are you here?" She glanced at Harvey, sitting at his feet.

"I'm keeping an eye on her and wanted to know why she came here first."

"Well, if you're going over there you can take her stuff."

He studied his sister. "You're usually very forgiving. Why are you so mad at her?"

"That same night, I had just asked her if we were the kind of friends who could tell each other anything and she said yes. I told her all my secrets. She didn't even trust me enough to tell me her real name."

"Let's go inside and sit down. I want to tell you what I discovered about Lizzy this evening." He led her to the sofa and sat down with her. Harvey searched for Mavis, but not finding her, laid down with his head on his paws and sighed.

Jason told Holly what Barker had found out from the Phoenix police department. "She came here because she was afraid. I don't think she meant to be hurtful."

"Then why are you following her?"

"At first it was because I thought her lies were suspicious, but now I'm just worried she's in danger. I have to go but give it some thought. I'll be around."

"Okay, thanks." Holly hugged him and walked him to the door.

Chapter 20

Confession

By the time Lizzy and Mavis finished eating, the sun had set, and the house was dark. "Why don't we go for a little walk? I've been sitting a lot." She put on Mavis' harness and realizing she didn't have her coat, pulled out a sweater to keep her warm. Then she put her own coat and boots back on. Her mind was churning as they walked and instead of going straight home, she made a detour to Theo's house, deciding to confront him. His lights were on, but when she rang the doorbell, he didn't answer. She waited and rang again. *That's strange.* She turned to leave and saw Holly on her front step, pounding on her door and shouting her name. She was going to call out to her, but the door opened, and someone yanked her inside. Standing frozen for a moment, trying to process what she had seen, Lizzy said, "Come on Mavis," and sprinted across the street, slipping and sliding on the ice. She quietly unlocked the door and unclipped the leash, listening. The voices were faint, coming from upstairs. Mavis ran toward the stairs, and she followed, bursting into her bedroom to find Holly sitting on the edge of the bed and Theo in front of the open safe. He raised a gun and fired at Mavis. Holly screamed.

Lizzy grabbed Mavis and ducked, pulling Holly off the bed, before moving the nightstand away from the wall. "Get behind the nightstand," she whispered, handing Mavis to her. Raising up onto her knees, Lizzy peered over the top of the bed. "Why are you here, Theo?"

Gone were the cardigan and the cane. This was Theo as she had seen him in his backyard. "Why are *you* here? I thought you were in jail."

"They had to let me go since I didn't do anything. I saw you burying something in your backyard and thought it was you that broke into my safe last time. What are you looking for?"

"I'm looking for what's rightfully mine. I spent twenty years locked away for stealing those coins and I want them back."

"The time you served doesn't cover the three people you've murdered since you've been out."

"You don't know anything. Where are the coins?"

"Whoever broke into the safe the first time took the little blue box, if that's what you're talking about, but it was locked so I don't know what was inside."

He pointed the gun at her. "You're lying. Where is it?"

"So you're going to up your count to six?"

"How do you figure six?" He squinted at her.

"Well, let's see." She counted on her fingers. "Helen and Fred Pederson, Mrs. Crocker, Me, Holly, and Mavis. That's six. Did I miss anyone?"

"Only two so far. Helen was an accident and dogs don't count."

"Yes, they do. Why Mrs. Crocker?"

"I should've. Stupid old busybody tried to blackmail me, if you can believe it."

"But why put her in my house? I thought we were friends."

"That was your first mistake. Money is my only friend. If I'd known you were going to be so much trouble, I could've just poisoned you at dinner."

"Did you really make all that food yourself?"

"Of course I did. They had some marvelous classes in the joint. Life skills they called 'em."

"Death skills maybe. You went in a thief and came out a killer. I still can't believe you killed Helen. You said you loved her. You were supposed to get married."

"You don't know anything about Helen, or my feelings. You should just keep your big mouth shut."

"If you didn't love her, why did you give her the box?"

"I did love her, and I trusted her, but I came back, and she had married someone else. Not only that, she told me she didn't know where the box was. You know why? That rat she married knew it was from me and he hid it. Now enough of this. Where is it?"

"I told you; someone broke into my safe and stole everything. If you didn't take it, what were you burying in your yard?"

"That stupid picture of me and Helen. I knew you recognized it."

Jason saw Lizzy running toward her house, so he followed. He walked through the open door and saw her sprinting up the stairs. Unsure whether he should follow or not, he loitered for a moment, until he heard the gunshot. Giving Harvey a hand gesture, he quietly mounted the stairs and stood behind the partially closed bedroom door. He couldn't see inside, but he could hear what they were saying and set his phone to record. Getting down on one knee next to Harvey, he put his hand on his back to reassure him. At some point Dennis arrived and stood next to him. He wanted to ask him why he was there, but his priority was keeping Harvey quiet. He became more and more impressed by Lizzy's quick thinking as she gradually got Theo to confess everything. After he told her he had buried a photograph, he said, "Now I have to figure out what to do about you two. If you don't know where the key or the box is, you're no use to me and I can't have you running around telling my secrets, can I?"

"Maybe we can help you find them."

"What else got stolen from your safe?"

"A gun, all my money, and my mother's jewelry."

"So you want to find the thief as much as I do."

"Absolutely. If I find him, he's dead."

"Okay. Maybe I'll let you help, but Holly and the mutt will have to go."

"We're a team. It's either all of us or none of us."

"Your choice. I can shoot three as easily as I can shoot two. In fact, if I shoot all of you, I can make it look like one of you got mad and shot the other two."

"Neither one of us would shoot the dog. No one will ever believe that. Unless…"

"What?"

"If you go downstairs and get my bottle of Malibu out of the fridge, we can all drink it then you can make it look like one of us did something crazy when we were drunk. That might work."

Theo was quiet for a moment. "I don't really see a downside to your plan. What's it look like?"

"It's a large, white glass bottle. Grab three glasses and the orange juice too."

"Got it."

<hr>

Harvey was fast. No sooner had Theo cleared the threshold, than he was lying on his back with a German Shepherd on his chest. He tried to lift his gun, but the pointed teeth resting against the skin of his neck quickly convinced him he should put it down. After relieving him of his weapon, reading him his rights, and cuffing him, Jason left him in the hall with Harvey. He went into the bedroom to check on Lizzy and Holly. Dennis followed.

"Whoa there," Jason said. Lizzy was helping Holly through the open window. When he entered the room, she put Mavis down and helped Holly back inside.

"When did you get here?" she asked.

"I followed you up. I've been outside the door the whole time."

"So you heard his confession?"

"I recorded it on my phone. Harvey's with him now."

"So's Mavis." Dennis smirked.

"What are you doing here?" Jason asked. Are you working with Theo?"

"No, but I do owe you an explanation."

"Let me call Barker to come pick him up, then we'll debrief." Jason paused. "Do you have Lizzy's gun?"

"Yes. You can have it back." He pulled the gun from the back of his waistband and handed it to her.

"And the other things?" Lizzy asked.

"Yeah, but not with me."

Jason frowned as he left the room to make his call and check on his prisoner.

<hr>

"Why don't you go downstairs and have a seat in the living room, Dennis. I want to talk to Lizzy in private."

"Or you two could go downstairs."

Holly put her hands on her hips. "Is this your house?"

"Dennis," Jason called from the hall. "Come out here, please."

Once he left the room, Holly shut the door and locked it. Facing Lizzy, she said, "You came over to apologize and I was rude and mean. Then you came in here and got between me and Theo. You put yourself in danger to protect me. Why did you do that?"

"I told you. You're the best friend I've ever had. I don't want anything to happen to you. Why were you banging on my door?"

"I talked to Jason and realized I was wrong. I'm sorry. I can't really explain why I was so upset, except maybe it was because I care so much."

"I'll tell you all about what happened to me when we get done with this police stuff. It's actually a relief to be able to be myself. My weird writer's brain is hard to explain when I can't tell anyone I'm a writer." Lizzy laughed. "Remember when we first ate together, and I left the table to make a note and said *That was a good one.*

"Then you said *What was?* and I said I had thought of a solution for a client?"

"Oh yeah. And sometimes you'll get this far away look in the middle of a conversation. Is that when you're thinking up a story?"

"Not a story necessarily, but a character or a conversation sometimes."

Holly took her hand. "I'm glad I know now. I'll understand you better."

Lizzy smiled. "It's a job only a best friend would want to take on." Looking at the closed door she asked, "What's going on with you and Dennis?"

"I don't know. After you were arrested, he came over and told me he loved me, but I'm not sure if he's a good guy or a bad guy, or if he'll even stick around."

"Maybe we'll find out during Jason's *debrief.* I want to know when he broke into my safe and why he had to take *everything.*"

Holly unlocked the door and gestured for Lizzy to go first. "Let's go find out."

⸙

Jason was sitting across from Dennis when they got downstairs. Harvey lay curled around Mavis in her bed. Lizzy looked at her tiny dog, still in her sweater. Shaking her head, she sat next to Jason. "Where do we start?" she asked, belatedly removing her coat.

"Let's start with Dennis so I can decide if he should even be a part of this conversation."

Dennis looked at him. "It might not make a lot of sense if we don't keep things in order. I can start by telling you why I'm really here and what I know, but then we need to proceed with how Lizzy figured out what was going on."

"Isn't that what I said? You start."

"I was hired to return those coins to their rightful owner, and I aim to do that.

"He's an old man now and they mean a lot to him."

"And who would that be?"

"The man Carson Davies stole them from; Robert Foster."

"You can verify that you're working for him?"

"Yes."

"Tell me the whole story and if we can verify the coins are his and he agrees, you can return them."

Dennis sighed. "Robert Foster is my grandfather. When Carson was sent to prison, he had law enforcement, employees, associates, keeping an eye out for those coins. If they had been bought, sold, or traded he would have heard about it. When I was twenty, about ten years into Carson's sentence, Grandfather made a deal with me. I wanted to be a fire fighter so he said he would fund my training if I would follow Carson when he was released and find his coins. I've been watching him for five years; ever since he moved here.

"And Mrs. Crocker was your aunt?"

"No. She was just a nosy neighbor."

"Then why did you want the journal?" Lizzy asked.

"I just wanted any information she had and to make sure there wasn't anything about me in there."

"What's so special about those coins?" Jason asked.

"My family has been collecting them for generations. They're the rarest and most elusive coins in existence, worth millions to the right investors. The collection isn't something that can be replaced. Grandfather is a wealthy man. He can buy anything he wants, but his coins have sentimental value as well. It's not just the money."

Dennis paused. "When Lizzy moved in, I tried to get close to her. Not just so I could nose around the house, but I wondered if she had anything to do with Carson. I thought maybe she was a friend or a relative, or maybe he had hired her to find the coins."

"What convinced you she wasn't working with him?" Jason asked.

"He was still breaking into the house. I had a lawn chair hidden in the trees out back. Sometimes I would follow him over here and just sit and watch. Unfortunately, Mrs. Fickle and Mrs. Crocker also liked to see what was going on at Lizzy's house. Ethel would actually creep up to the windows and look inside. One night Lizzy saw her and screamed bloody murder. I've never seen that woman run so fast."

"Did Mrs. Crocker see you watching and try to blackmail you?"

"Yeah. And I gave her money and tried to warn her that blackmail was not a safe profession. She thought I was threatening her, but I was talking about Carson. He had already killed and wouldn't worry about one more."

"Weren't you concerned about Lizzy's safety?"

"Not until he killed Mrs. Crocker."

"Why did you break into her safe?"

"Probably for the same reason Carson did. I thought she might have found the coins."

"Where are they now?"

"I asked Pearl to take care of them for me."

Jason's eyebrows rose.

"Officer Rice."

"Is she looking after the journal too? It's not in the evidence room."

Lizzy wanted to wipe that little smile right off Dennis' face, but Jason did it for her. "Tampering with evidence is a punishable offense," he said.

"I was going to give it back. Do you have the key to the box?"

"Yes, I do. Helen Pederson gave it to Mrs. Fickle for safekeeping."

Turning to Lizzy, Jason asked, "How did you figure everything out?"

"It was Mavis really. She found the coins and the picture of Helen and Carson. Theo had the same photo at his house, by the way.

"She started chewing up my research about the robbery and she hated Theo. I was kind of wondering if she saw him kill Mr. Pederson."

"How did you know he killed the Pedersons?"

"I was guessing. Dottie told me Helen died suddenly while eating dinner with her husband and a friend and I thought of poison. Remember Theo said it was a mistake? He probably meant to kill her husband, and I think he did, six months later."

Jason nodded. "Someone bought a plane ticket in his name, but he wasn't on the flight."

"I also saw Theo digging in his back yard and he looked much younger than he usually acted. Maybe if you take Mavis and search his house you can find the mate to the glove she found."

"The glove?"

"The second time he broke into my house, Mavis chased him outside and came back with a winter glove. I put it in the closet. Even though he admitted to breaking in, that would be evidence, right? And Mavis could probably dig up the photo he buried as well."

Jason nodded. "I'll need you all to sign statements, and Dennis, I'll need you to bring the box and the journal in, then we'll call your grandfather and verify your story."

"I have one more question," Lizzy said. "Why were you acting so out of character after Mrs. Crocker died?"

"What do you mean?"

"Your usual charm was gone. You were making people mad. You knocked that elderly man over at the party and wouldn't let Stacy help him up. You tried to kick Mavis." Lizzy frowned at the memory.

"I didn't realize it was so obvious. My grandfather was putting pressure on me and my wallet was missing and your house had become a crime scene so I couldn't get to the box. Then I drank too much at the party. I didn't know what I was doing."

Lizzy could tell Holly wanted to ask him something too, but she kept her lips firmly sealed. "Did you have a question, Holly?"

"Yes, but it's off topic. I'll ask later."

"Why don't you go ahead and ask now? I'm sure we'd all like to hear the answer."

"I-I'd like to know if you cared about any of the women you used. Stacy…Pearl…me? Or were you just doing what you had to do?"

"That *is* kind of personal. Maybe we could discuss that in private."

"I don't think so. If you can't give me a straight answer, I don't want to lose any more sleep over it." Holly leveled her gaze at him and waited.

"It's complicated," he said. "I was doing what I had to do, but I always thought you and me would end up together."

Holly was shaking her head. "That's not the way it works. I've learned a lot about love and trust from Lizzy, and this is not it."

"That's…disappointing. Maybe you'll change your mind after a couple months of snow."

"Ha. He said something like that to me before. You need some new material," Lizzy said.

"Well." Jason stood. "I think that's our cue. We should get back to the station. Harve?"

Harvey opened his eyes but didn't move.

"Is it okay if I leave him here for now? He was so good earlier, when we were waiting in the hall, and he seems happy where he is."

"That's fine." Lizzy smiled. "My only concern is potty time, but I suppose he'll stick close when I take Mavis out?"

"I think so. I wouldn't leave him here if I wasn't sure he'd behave. Come on, Dennis, let's get a move on."

Chapter 21

Treasure Box

Jason drove Dennis back to the station and called for Officer Rice. When she entered his office, she carefully refrained from looking at Dennis.

"I would like you to bring me the blue box and the journal please," Jason said.

"I…" She glanced at Dennis, who nodded. "Yes, Sir." She turned and left the office.

"You understand she'll lose her job over this," Jason said.

"Yes." Dennis' face held no expression.

"Doesn't that bother you?"

"Believe it or not, I didn't ask her to do any of the things she did. Manipulation is something I'm very familiar with. I can recognize it immediately and I have no respect for people who wield it. My grandfather is an expert."

"You're telling me Rice was trying to manipulate you?"

He nodded. "We had a little tryst, and she wanted more."

"That's hard for me to believe. She's always been such a rule follower."

"When she released me, she gave me her house key. Then she called and told me you were looking for me. Her help was convenient, but I didn't ask for it and can't take responsibility for her decisions."

"But you asked her to look after the coins."

"Not even that. She offered."

"Will she verify that?"

"If she's honest. I have no idea how far she'll go to save her job."

"Was all that stuff you told me about Holly a bunch of lies?"

161

"No, I admire her very much. I won't pursue her; she's too good for me."

Jason thought Holly might be just what Dennis needed, but he wasn't about to encourage him. *I have to stay out of it. I don't want to be responsible for her misery.*

Rice returned and placed the blue box and the journal on the desk. "Will that be all, Sir?"

"I'll need your badge and your gun. You're suspended pending an internal investigation."

She glanced at Dennis before silently handing them to Jason. Then she turned and left the office.

Jason lifted the box. "It's small but heavy. How many coins do you think it holds?"

"I have no idea. I haven't seen the collection since I was a child, and the coins weren't in a box at that time."

Jason pulled out a key and inserted it into the keyhole, turning it and opening the box. Then he laughed. He laughed so hard, his eyes watered and his stomach cramped.

"What?" Dennis demanded. "What's so funny? Let me see." He held out his hand.

Jason held out the box and finally pulled himself together, his laughter subsiding to an occasional snicker.

Dennis took it and looked inside. He wasn't laughing. It was filled with pennies and a small note on top read, *Better luck next time.* "I don't know why you think this is funny," he said quietly. "Now I'll have to start all over again. I was watching Theo because I thought he knew where the coins were, but he doesn't know either."

"I think it's time to call your grandfather. Do you have his number?"

Dennis nodded and pulled it up on his phone.

After Jason and Dennis left, Lizzy and Holly remained in the living room with the dogs. Holly was silent for so long, Lizzy asked, "Are you okay?"

"I'm just…I can't believe Dennis is such a fake. I really thought we were going to end up together. I'm so disappointed I can't even cry. The things he said."

Lizzy walked around to her chair and got on her knees, hugging her; then the tears came. Holly cried for a long time. Lizzy's legs went numb. Mavis whined. The doorbell rang but she didn't move. She stayed by Holly's side and hugged her until the crying tapered off.

"Who do you suppose was at the door?" Holly asked finally, wiping her eyes with her sleeve. She sniffed. "I hope it wasn't important."

"You are important. Anything else can wait. Let me get you a tissue." Holding on to the coffee table, she pulled herself up and waited briefly for the blood to return to her legs.

Holly grasped her hand before she could walk away. "Thank you for being here for me."

"I'll always be here for you. I learned my lesson."

"What lesson?"

"That a good friend is precious and has to be taken care of." Lizzy smiled. "You and Mavis saved me from myself." She walked to the kitchen counter and grabbed the box of tissues.

When the bell rang again, she handed Holly the box and said, "I'll see who's at the door." She wondered why Mavis wasn't barking.

Lizzy opened the door to Holly's mother. One of Mavis' previous caretakers, she didn't get the guard-dog treatment. "Where's Holly?" she asked as she rushed into the house.

"Right here," Lizzy gestured.

Mrs. Schneider wasn't listening. "Sage is gone," she said. "She took the minivan and disappeared."

"Why would she do that? Couldn't she just ask for a ride?"

"It must have something to do with her husband. We should call Jason," Holly said.

"Isn't he busy right now?"

"He's not too busy to hear this. It'll only take a minute."

She watched as Holly picked up her phone and called. Her eyes got round, and she said, "No. Nothing like that. We're fine." She paused to listen. "It's Mrs. Fickle. She took Mom's car and left. Is Mr. Fickle still in custody?" Pausing again, she said, "Okay. I'll tell her. Thanks. Bye."

"He said not to worry, Mom. He'll check on it."

"Did he say anything else?"

"No, just that he was busy. You were right, but he seemed glad to have the information anyway. Is anyone hungry? I missed supper."

"I have left over frozen pizza."

"That'll work. You want some, mom?"

"No. I need to get home. I've got your dad's car, and he always thinks I'm going to dent it. Don't forget about the Ball Friday night. I'm counting on you to be there."

"I almost forgot. We've had so much going on. You can pick out a different dress, Lizzy, since yours got all snagged up."

"Do we have to go to another party?"

"Yes, we do, but not until day after tomorrow. You will be my date and keep me from being sad."

"You should be ashamed, using guilt as a weapon."

"It's a life-long skill I inherited from my mom." Holly grinned. "Don't worry. You'll have a marvelous time."

<hr>

Jason dialed Robert Foster's number on his office phone and waited. Mr. Foster answered on the fifth ring.

"Foster," he said.

"Hello, Mr. Foster. This is Captain Jason Schneider from the Harperstown police department. I'm calling to verify your connection with Dennis Wright, who is with me here."

"Ah, yes. I've been meaning to call him. Could you please let him know the coins have been recovered and his services are no longer needed?"

"Recovered?"

"Yes, someone returned them to me this afternoon."

"May I ask who?"

"She didn't give a name, but she was an older woman with a long grey braid."

"Did she say where she got them?"

"No, and I didn't ask. I am just relieved to have them back."

"Would you like to speak with Dennis?"

"No, not at the moment. Just pass on my message please."

"I will. Thank you very much and congratulations."

Disconnecting, he looked at Dennis. "Someone returned the coins."

"I gathered that from your conversation. I'm not sure how I feel about that. On the one hand, I don't have to start over again, but on the other, I've spent the last fifteen years trying to find them. I'm suddenly a free man. I'll have to think about that." He gazed at Jason. "Can I go now?"

"Yes. You'll need to testify at Carson Davies' trial. I don't think Lizzy's going to press charges, but you should return her belongings."

"I will. I need to talk to her anyway." He stood. "I think you should let her read the journal. It's not about her, but I think it might speak to her. She's an interesting lady."

Jason agreed, but those thoughts were personal, and he kept them to himself. He stood as well and shook Dennis' hand. "Stay out of trouble," he said.

"I may have misjudged you, Schneider. You're all right in my book."

Exhausted, Lizzy sat in the living room with the dogs after Holly left. She felt ambivalent about her first night at home, her first night alone since Mavis moved in. *At least she's still here with me.* She smiled at her little dog, still curled up with Harvey. "Do you two need to go outside?"

Mavis thumped her tail twice and Harvey's head went up as there was a knock at the door.

"Who is it?" Lizzy called.

"It's me. Jason."

She glanced at the clock. Midnight. Opening the door, she said, "Just in time. I was getting ready to take our friends out to do their business."

He handed her Mrs. Crocker's journal. "Dennis said I should let you read this. Since it was never logged as evidence and only Dennis has read it, perhaps you can let me know if she wrote anything pertinent."

"Why did he think I should read it?"

"I'm not sure. He said it might *speak to you*, whatever that means. Maybe you can tell me when you're finished."

"Deal." She hesitated. "Is it all over now? I won't have any more break ins or dead bodies?"

"It's all over."

"You'll probably think I'm strange, but I don't feel safe here anymore."

"We'll call you eccentric," he chuckled, "but I understand. If you like, I could sleep on the couch tonight and help you get an alarm installed tomorrow."

"Would you?" Lizzy fought against imminent tears. She hated showing any kind of weakness, but the last week had worn her down to the point of collapse.

Jason gave her a hug. "I would be glad to, and Harve will be pleased. Come on Harve, let's go outside. Mavis. You too."

Mavis got up first, wagging her tail. Harvey followed.

Jason waited for Lizzy to put her coat back on, then opened the front door, and they all went outside. Lizzy shivered. "Is this snow ever going to melt?"

"It has been melting during the day."

"But then it snows again. I feel like I've been living in an alternate reality ever since Mrs. Crocker was murdered."

"In a way you have. Now everything can go back to normal."

Do I want it to go back to normal? It's nice having friends but my writing has suffered. "What?"

"Harve and Mavis are ready to go back inside."

"Oh. Sorry. Can I get you anything before we retire? I have a blanket and an extra toothbrush."

"That would be great. Can I build a fire?"

"Sure. Just make yourself at home. I feel so guilty making you do this."

"I'm pretty sure I offered." He smiled then went to work starting the fire while she went upstairs for the blanket and toothbrush.

When she returned, she thanked him and said goodnight to Mavis before going back up to her room. It felt strange sleeping without her little dog, especially since she'd been away from her the previous night. She got into bed and lay with her eyes open for a few minutes, then heard scratching on her door. Grinning happily, she opened the door to find not only Mavis, but Harvey too. "Hm. I guess my room is party central tonight." She left her door open for the first time and got back into bed. Mavis curled up next to her and Harvey lay at her feet.

Chapter 22

She Wouldn't Miss It

Lizzy slept for ten hours. When she woke, she was alone in her room and the house seemed unusually still. *Where's Mavis? Maybe the trick is leaving the door open.* She rolled over and sat up. Sunlight streamed through her window. Her stomach growled. Once she was dressed, she went downstairs to investigate. Jason's blanket was neatly folded on the sofa. Lured into the kitchen by the smell of freshly brewed coffee, she saw his note on the table.

> *I hope you slept well. Harvey wouldn't leave without Mavis so*
> *she's riding shotgun today. I hope you don't mind. I made*
> *coffee and got you sweets from the Hummingbird. I also put in*
> *a call to the home security company I use. They should be there*
> *around eleven.*

Pouring herself a cup of coffee, Lizzy peeked into the paper bag on the counter and smiled. The selection reminded her of her joke about getting one of everything. *How can I decide?* She started with the cranberry-orange scone. Her favorite.

Holly showed up in time to share breakfast. She joined Lizzy at the table and asked, "Where's Mavis?"

"Jason has her. It's like shared custody or something."

Holly giggled. "We have to decorate your house, or Santa won't know to visit."

"But it's only for one day."

"You can keep them up for a few weeks since we're getting a late start. I'll help. It won't take long. Then I'll bake while you work."

"I need more coffee first."

"Okay, I'll go up and get the box of decorations."

"Slave driver." She poured more coffee then went to answer the door again.

Two technicians from the Ace Security company introduced themselves. After explaining her options, they began the installation. Holly returned with the decorations and took them out front, where Lizzy joined her. "What all's in there?" she asked.

Holly pulled out window clings, lights, and oversized candy canes. "This should be enough for this year. There's more, but you're right; we're starting late. The Pedersons already have little hooks for the lights, so it'll be easy."

Christmas had never been on Lizzy's radar, other than buying presents for William. She enjoyed hanging the lights with Holly, who was just a big kid. As they were finishing up she said, "What about the presents I ordered? I haven't got them yet."

"I forgot to tell you. You got some deliveries yesterday. Also, you know those guys who met with Mr. Fickle? All the missing presents were in their van, still wrapped and everything."

"That's great."

"Come on over and pick out a dress for tonight, then I'll help you carry your packages back."

"Is there that much?"

"I suspect you bought out Amazon."

"Well, since I'll be spending Christmas Eve with your family, I wanted to be prepared."

"That's super sweet but they won't be expecting gifts."

"Even better."

Lizzy found the perfect dress at Holly's, a fitted, shimmering white gown with beads and sequins.

"It's beautiful." Lizzy ran her hand over the fabric.

"I have a long white wig too."

"What are you going to wear?"

"I can wear the same dress I wore to Dottie's party. It's very Christmasy."

After they carried the dress and the boxes across the street, Holly said, "I still have some wrapping to do. I'll be back in a couple of hours, then we can have dinner."

Once Holly and the security techs left, Lizzy poured another cup of coffee and sat down with Ethel Crocker's journal. Her handwriting was neat and easy to read. As Lizzy read, she felt increasingly sad. The entries began after Ethel's husband died. She suddenly found herself alone and the women she thought were her friends turned their backs on her. Her entries became increasingly disillusioned and bitter. When Helen died, she wrote,

> *My last real friend died last night. Now I am truly alone. It*
> *doesn't matter; friends are overrated. I always wondered about*
> *Theo Hoffmeyer. I'd bet money he killed her. I'll be keeping*
> *my eye on him.*

She didn't write a lot, or often, but made notes when someone in town did or said something she thought was suspect. When she started seeing Dave Moon she wrote more.

> *I finally have a friend. I should feel guilty about loving a*
> *married man, but I don't. He is such a wonderful man, and*
> *his wife treats him like a dog. Finding someone I can trust*
> *and talk to has made a huge difference in my life. I didn't*
> *realize how lonely I've been.*

"Oh, no," Lizzy said out loud. "He's going to crush her." She continued reading. Ethel still made occasional notes about the people in town, including a vague entry about a suspected relationship between Stacy and Coral.

> *Those two got out of the backseat of Coral's car, looking*
> *around and straightening their clothes, giggling. Stacy looked*
> *nervous when she saw me. Coral tried to kiss her, but she*
> *pushed her away and nodded in my direction. Very*
> *interesting.*

Just as Lizzy reached the entry about Dave's betrayal, she was interrupted by a knock on her front door. It's like buy one get one at the mall. She put the journal aside and got up to answer the door, surprised to discover Mrs. Fickle.

"Hello, dear. I hope I'm not disturbing you."

"Of course not. When did you get back?"

Mrs. Fickle chuckled. "You heard about that, did you? I got back this morning." Taking Lizzy's arm, she said, "I need to talk to you about something. You can keep a secret, right?"

"Usually, unless it'll hurt someone."

"Looking left and right, Mrs. Fickle said, "Can we go inside and talk? I don't want anyone to see us."

"Come in. Would you like some coffee? Oh, wait, you don't drink coffee. Tea?"

"No, I'm fine. You have some though." She sat at the kitchen table and pulled out a key ring. "Percy told me who you are. He carries your books in his shop. I need to share my secret with someone, in case something happens to me. Helen Pederson was my best friend, and she knew, but she's gone now. I figure it could help you, so I want you to be my one person."

"Now I'm very curious."

"You're hiding out, right?"

Lizzy nodded.

"Let me see. How should I begin?" Mrs. Fickle tapped her finger against pursed lips. "Let's start with the secret passage. Decades ago, Helen and I had a tunnel built between our two homes. It goes from your basement to ours. No one knows about it except the two of us. The keys to each side are here on the ring."

"Will you show me?"

"Yes, but later. I have an escape route, and you can use it too. There's more but I have to go now. I still have Thelma's minivan."

"Why did you take the minivan? She was really worried."

"I had something I had to do." She paused. "I guess I can tell you."

Lizzy waited for her to continue.

"Before Helen died, she was afraid for her husband. A man named Carson Davies had given her a small, locked box before he went to prison, and he wanted it back.

She found out the coins he stole were in the box, so she gave them to me for safe keeping. I had to return them to their rightful owner."

"Why now?"

"Percy's in trouble and I didn't want him or my cousin to find out about the coins. They're worth enough to kill for."

Lizzy sat very still.

"I can see I've shocked you. Keep those keys safe and I'll explain everything later."

She stood abruptly and hurried off, leaving Lizzy stunned. She looked in the bakery bag and selected a chocolate croissant. Something was niggling in the back of her mind, but she couldn't remember what it was. She frowned and picked up Ethel's journal.

***

Holly said she'd be back in two hours but when it got too dark to read, Lizzy turned on the lights and looked at the clock. Six o'clock. She tried to call but Holly's phone went straight to voicemail, so she headed across the street to see what happened. *Maybe she fell asleep.* She rang the gong but didn't get an answer, so she called Jason.

"Schneider."

"Do you know where Holly is?"

"No, why? Aren't I supposed to come over at seven?"

"She said she'd be back for lunch, hours ago. I'm at her door now but she isn't home. Where could she be?"

"I'll check with Mom and be over soon. Should I bring supper?"

"That would be great. I haven't eaten anything except the pastries you left, and Holly might not have eaten either. I feel like I missed something last night and I'm worried. Let me know if you find her."

"I will. I'm sure she's fine."

Lizzy disconnected and stood for a moment. *Where are you, Holly?*

At seven, Jason arrived with pizza, wings, and beer. "Have you heard anything yet?"

"No. Your mom hasn't heard from her?"

"I couldn't get ahold of her."

"Mrs. Fickle stopped by on her way back." Her head was beginning to pound. "Where are Mavis and Harvey?"

"I left them in the car for now. Let's have a bite to eat, then I'll take them with me to check out her house."

They sat at the kitchen table and Jason opened the pizza box, then as Lizzy ate a slice of pizza, chewing slowly, it came to her. *Dennis.* She put her pizza down, half eaten, and said, "Where's Dennis?"

Jason's hand stopped in midair.

"He said he couldn't search for the blue box after Mrs. Crocker was killed but when did he break into the safe? You should check his house. If she's not there, check her house. She wouldn't miss this for the world."

"I'm on it. I'll be back soon." He stood and pulled out his radio as he headed for the door.

Lizzy started a fire and finished her slice of pizza, worrying about Holly and wondering how long Jason would be.

⁕

Jason radioed Barker as he left Lizzy's. Deciding to try Holly's house while he waited, he opened her front door with his key and flipped the light switch. Nothing. He tried the kitchen switch too, with no luck. Using his flashlight, he found a pile of wrapped gifts on her kitchen table. A tray of sandwiches sat on the counter. The knife, cutting board, and a partially sliced cucumber were strewn around. *What happened here?*

He radioed Barker again and instructed him to meet him at Holly's and not to ring the bell.

When Barker arrived, he told him to wait and went out to his cruiser to get the dogs. He didn't bother with harnesses and leashes, just said, "Come on. Help me find Holly." He opened the front door and Mavis shot past him, Harvey on her heels. She dashed into the kitchen first, then to a door beneath the staircase. Whining and scratching at the door, she looked back at Jason and barked.

The door was locked, so he slid a credit card down the crack along the door jam and opened it. Harvey, ever the gentleman, lowered his body so Mavis could climb on his back, before carefully carrying her down the wooden steps. Jason flipped the light switch, but nothing happened, so he and Barker descended using their flashlights. Mavis yelped and Dennis yelled. "Get your dog off me." His voice was considerably higher than usual. Grateful the homes in this neighborhood were a similar layout, Jason found the breaker box and restored the power. Sitting in the corner, Holly's mouth was gagged, and her hands tied behind her. Dennis was on his back with Harvey's bared teeth around his neck. When the lights went on and he could see how close he was to death, his eyes rolled back, and he passed out.

"Good boy," Jason told Harvey on his way across the room. He removed Holly's gag, asking, "What happened?" as he worked on releasing her wrists.

"He came over and tried to convince me we belong together. When I told him no, he grabbed me and tried to kiss me. I had the knife in my hand and told him to back off. Then he got mad. He took the knife and threw it, then smacked me. I fell and must have hit my head. When I came to, I was here in the dark. That was so scary when you guys came down. I was worried he would sneak up on you, then I heard a yelp. I think he kicked Mavis. I guess he made Harvey mad. Look at him. He's in killer mode."

Dennis opened his eyes and Harvey growled deep in his throat. Jason chuckled. "You're going to have to ease up, Harve, so I can get the cuffs on." Dennis gulped.

"Do you mind explaining why you thought kidnapping Holly would be a good idea?"

Dennis didn't move.

"Release," he told Harvey. "Go take care of Mavis."

Harvey reluctantly removed his teeth from Dennis' neck, but remained standing over him, his legs stiff.

"Now answer me, Dennis. What's the big idea?"

"She's mine. We belong together."

"I don't think kidnapping someone is the way to get them to love you." Jason snapped on the cuffs. Read him his rights Barker. Jason called for an ambulance, then called Lizzy.

"I don't need to go to the hospital," Holly insisted.

"At least let the paramedics check you out."

⁕⸺◦⟨○⟩◦⸺⁕

When Jason called, Lizzy grabbed her coat and ran across the street. Holly's door was unlocked, and the lights were on. "Hello? Where is everyone?"

"Down here," she heard, noticing the open door below the stairs.

Peering down into the basement, she jogged down the steps and threw her arms around Holly. "Dennis killed Ethel Crocker," she said.

"Didn't Theo confess to killing her?" Jason asked.

"No. He said, *I should have*. Something was bothering me, but I couldn't remember exactly what it was. Then I remembered. Dennis said he was out of sorts because Mrs. Crocker was murdered in my house, and he couldn't get in to search anymore. When did he break into my safe?"

"Shut up," Dennis growled.

"We only have your word for what time you met with her. You said she had her phone and that you lost your wallet.

"I think she caught you sneaking out of the house and threatened you. You strangled her and drug her inside, put the cash and your wallet in her pocket, took her phone upstairs and hid it in my laundry basket, and broke into my safe. Then, you stabbed her with one of my kitchen knives to put more suspicion on me. You took your time. You even closed and locked my back door when you left."

"You're just showing off. We know you have a great imagination, but this isn't fiction. You don't get to just make things up," Dennis said.

Jason was nodding. "That's how you know she's a writer. You saw the book on her desk. We based your whole alibi on the time you told us and your wallet in her pocket. Very clever."

"You don't believe her. You can't convict someone based on a crackpot author's plot."

"No, but we can convict you with the medical examiner's report and Mrs. Fickle's statement."

"One more thing," Lizzy said with dawning realization. "He came over to borrow butter the night before, so he had a chance to drug Mavis."

"And you, actually," Jason said. "Holly gave me a heads up and we had your drink tested."

Lizzy gaped at him.

"Take him to the station Barker and get him processed. I'll be there shortly."

Holly checked on Mavis while the paramedics checked on her, everyone receiving a clean bill of health. "Have we missed the ball? How did you know where to find me?"

"We haven't and we didn't. Lizzy suggested I check with Dennis, but I decided to come over here while I was waiting for Barker. When the lights were out, I brought in the dogs. Mavis found you."

"Such a good puppy." Holly hugged her.

"I have work to do now," Jason said, "but I'll meet you at the ball, if you're still up for it."

"I'm up for it."

"Can Harvey stay with Mavis while we're out?"

"Of course," Lizzy said. "Grab your dress Holly and let's go over to my house. Jason brought pizza, if you've still got an appetite."

"Thank you both. I don't know what would have happened if you hadn't found me."

Chapter 23

Christmas Ball

When she put on the gown, Lizzy thought it was the most beautiful thing she'd ever seen. Her hair didn't do it justice, so she was grateful for the wig. Holly did her makeup, and she felt like royalty. "Are you sure you're okay to go out and socialize?"

"The Christmas Ball is more than just socializing. It's a time when we celebrate together as a community. No matter who you are or what kind of traditions you grew up with, you have family around you. This is an opportunity to embrace something bigger than ourselves. Plus—my mom would kill me if I didn't show up." Holly giggled.

"That's a nice sentiment, especially for someone like me."

"Don't you have any family at all?"

"My father died on Christmas day and my mom took me to my aunt's house and left me there. She didn't want me, but didn't know how to get rid of me, so I was kind of on my own."

"How old were you?"

"Thirteen. I got a job, but if I bought myself anything, like new clothes, my cousin took them. I tested out of high school and moved out as soon as I turned sixteen."

"Where's your mom?"

She shook her head. "I don't know. She might be dead. I wanted to be a famous writer so she could find me, but that hasn't worked out too well either."

"We're your family now." Holly hugged her. "Me and my family and our community. We're your family."

Blinking rapidly, Lizzy was touched. "Have I told you you're the best friend ever?"

"You have," Holly said with a smile. "Are you ready to go?"

"You bet'cha," Lizzy mimicked the local slang, making her giggle. "Do you think we can trust these two criminals?"

"They look pretty cozy. I think they'll be fine here together." She looked at her watch. "Barker said he'll pick us up. Why don't we put on our boots and change into our shoes when we get there?"

<hr>

Although she had seen the community center from the street, Lizzy was dazzled by the lavish decorations inside. The events room was transformed into a magical world of glittering red, white, and green. "Does it look the same every year?" she asked.

"No, a committee is elected each year, and they're in charge of deciding on a theme and drumming up volunteers to make it happen."

Holly wandered off so Lizzy helped herself to snacks and punch and watched arriving guests greet their friends and neighbors. Stacy and Coral entered together. Coral, sporting a new pixie cut, wore a simple green dress. Stacy, wearing a ball gown, held her hand. Lizzy felt her heart swell. She was so proud of them for feeling free to be themselves. She walked over to them and gave Stacy a hug. "You two look great," she said.

"Thanks," Stacy whispered. "My dad's going to have a fit."

"It's always better to be who you really are, than to pretend to be something you're not. It might be difficult at first, but in the long run you'll be happier. I learned that the hard way."

"I'm so sorry about everything. Coral said she thought you were beautiful, and I lost my head. I wish I hadn't messed up your hair."

"Water under the bridge. It'll grow back." Lizzy smiled.

"I'm sorry too," Coral said. "I wasn't very nice in the grocery, but I was worried you would retaliate. I don't have anything against you."

"So what was going on with Dennis?"

"He and I were putting on a show," Stacy said. "We were helping each other put on a façade."

"It bugged me a lot," Coral said. "I'm glad it's over."

"D-day. Dad's on his way over."

"I'll take off then. Good luck," Lizzy said.

Dressed in an elf costume, Dottie slid her arm through Lizzy's and smiled. "Are you enjoying yourself, dear?"

"This is quite a party."

"I was on the decorations committee this year. Perhaps you'd like to help us plan for next year. We have a lot of fun. Come meet the others." Dottie guided her over to a group of women, some of them Lizzy recognized from the bakery and the grocers.

Heart pounding, Lizzy expected a cold suspicious reception, but all the women greeted her warmly.

"We heard about how you saved Holly and helped the police solve Ethel's murder. You're so brave," one of the ladies said.

"And you write books. Is that how you figured out who did it?"

"We've never had anyone famous here. How do you like Harperstown?"

Lizzy stared at Dottie in horror. *Where do these women get their information? How do I stop them from spreading it?*

"Dottie," she whispered. "It's supposed to be a secret."

"There are no secrets here." She turned to her friends. "The best part is that Lizzy is letting us share her secret and if anyone from out of town comes looking for her, we'll know something they don't." She wiggled her brows.

Holly left Lizzy to make friends, but she kept an eye on her. She saw her speak with Stacy and Coral, then she filled a plate with snacks and stood in the corner. Mrs. Fickle approached Lizzy and spoke for a few minutes, then Dottie introduced her to some of her friends.

Jason arrived in a tuxedo and stood watching her as well. He approached her when she wandered off from the group, holding out a hand and leading her onto the dance floor. Holly felt a little jealous as she watched them dance but knew in her heart she was wrong. Neither of them had been lucky in love and they were perfect for each other. As she watched, lulled into a peaceful state of acceptance, she saw Lizzy stiffen and pull away. Jason's face turned a deep shade of crimson as he spoke. The two of them stepped away from each other and stared, before turning and walking in opposite directions. *What happened?*

She found Lizzy in the women's restroom, leaning against the counter, her hands holding on with a death grip. She stared at herself in the mirror with intense eyes, her lips pressed together.

"What happened?" Holly asked.

"Did you know he had Barker ask the Phoenix police department about me?"

"Well, yes. That's how they found out what happened to you."

"Don't you know what that means?"

"No. What?"

"It means there's an official record of me living here. I'll have to move again. This is why I didn't want anyone to know."

The muscles in Lizzy's face and shoulders were so stiff Holly thought she might hurt herself. Her eyes were shiny with unshed tears and her lower lip trembled. "I need to leave."

"I'll come with you," Holly said.

"No. Please. I need to be alone. I'll talk to you tomorrow."

Holly watched her turn and rush out of the ladies' room, wishing she knew how to help.

Thoughts raced through Lizzy's head as she walked home alone. She was only partially aware of the gentle snowflakes drifting down around her. Try as she might, she was unable to stave off the panic welling up inside. *How long will it take them to show up in Harperstown? Will my new friends help me keep my secret?* The short burst of a siren and flashing red and blue lights reflecting off the snow warned Lizzy she was no longer alone. The crunch of boots followed her as she picked up her pace.

"Lizzy. Wait up."

The voice didn't belong to Jason. *Am I disappointed?* She supposed she was, a little. When she stopped and turned, Officer Barker was jogging toward her. "Let me give you a ride home. You're not dressed for this weather."

"I just want to be alone."

"I understand. You don't have to talk if you don't want to, but at least let me make sure you get home safe."

Shrugging in defeat, Lizzy allowed him to lead her to the cruiser. Once she got settled, Barker put the car in gear and drove slowly toward her house.

"You know, we weren't trying to cause you problems when we ran the background check. You never told anyone what you were hiding from, so we had no idea."

"Would you have believed me if I told you?"

"Probably not," he admitted.

Leaning her head back and staring at the roof of the car, Lizzy sighed. "I don't want to have to move again. I like it here."

"It was really bad, huh?"

"I was afraid to leave my house, or even open my door. One man pretended to be a delivery guy. He set a package on my doorstep and hid around the corner."

"How did you escape?"

"My lawyer created an LLC for me and helped me buy a plane ticket and my house here. Then he helped sneak me out of my house and change my appearance." Lizzy smiled wanly at the memory. "It was very cloak and dagger."

Pulling up in front of her house, Barker said, "The captain isn't a bad guy. We'll do everything we can to make sure you're safe."

"Thank you. I appreciate that." She said goodnight and got out of the cruiser. Letting herself into her house, she reset the alarm and sat on the sofa in the dark. The streetlight outside reflected off Harvey and Mavis' eyes as they watched her.

She sat there a long time, lost in her thoughts. The panic gradually subsided as she made up her mind. *I don't want to run away again. This is my home, my new family. I am not a victim. I'll fight for it this time.* Mavis jumped up on the sofa and laid down next to her, with her chin on her lap. "Thank you, Mavis." She rubbed her little dog's ears and watched the snow fall outside her window.

Chapter 24

Christmas Eve

With a strong sense of déjà vu, Lizzy opened her eyes to the sight of Mavis' snout in her face. "Ahrooerer," she said, and licked Lizzy's nose. She glanced at the clock and groaned. "It's only six, puppy. Why're you awake?" Mavis barked and nudged her hand. "Okay, I'm coming." When she placed her on the floor, Harvey jumped off the foot of the bed. "Oh, good morning, Harvey. I forgot you were here. Give me a second." She had to keep in mind how cold it was outside now that her heater worked. Slipping on sweatsuit bottoms and a hoodie, she let the dogs out the front door and noticed gratefully that someone had shoveled a patch of grass. Harvey was quicker, but both dogs took care of business and ran for the door. Following them into the kitchen, she gave them both kibble and started a pot of coffee. "I hope the mini bits are okay for you, Harvey. I don't have any big dog food." She grabbed a piece of leftover pizza and headed for her desk. Life was back to normal, and she planned to write. *It's been much too long.*

Harvey and Mavis lay in the dog bed and Lizzy sat in front of her laptop with a cup of coffee. All was quiet. No interruptions. She stared at the screen and couldn't remember where she left off. Shaking her head, she went back to the beginning of her manuscript and started the read aloud feature. She leaned back, listening to her story as she drank her coffee and before long, she was back on track. Lizzy smiled as she typed. She loved her main character, Rachael. She was smart and adventurous and fun to write. After several solid hours of writing, Mavis ran to the door barking and the doorbell rang. Still cautious, Lizzy said, "Who is it?"

"It's Holly."

Lizzy pulled the door open and smiled. "Did you get some sleep?"

"I did. I was that tired. Did you get some writing done?"

"Yep. Lots. Mavis woke me up at six. I've been eating pizza too. Want a piece?"

"I'll get in trouble if I ruin my appetite. We eat early on Christmas Eve."

"Is that what everyone wears?"

"Yep. I brought you one too."

Holly handed her the gaudiest Christmas sweater she had ever seen. "Seriously?"

"You bet'cha." She laughed. "That's my best one."

"Augh."

"Go put it on. Dad's hungry."

"Okay. Any update on Dennis?"

"Jason didn't bring it up. I think he was trying not to upset me."

"Does talking about him upset you?"

"I was equal parts angry and scared last night. I think it cured me. But when I close my eyes, I can still feel the fear. I can taste the gag in my mouth, and I remember the darkness and the movement around me. It was terrible." She trembled.

Lizzy hugged her. "I'm sorry you had to go through that, but I'm glad you're okay. He's locked up now and can't hurt you anymore."

"Do you want to talk about last night? You were pretty upset."

"Barker gave me a ride home and talked to me a little. I've decided not to run away this time."

"Good. Remember, we're family. If you're in trouble, we'll rally around."

"You're the best, despite the sweater."

"I brought Mavis' coat back, so I'll get her bundled up while you change.

⁕⁕⁖⟳⬥⟲⁖⁕⁕

Outside, once they had navigated Lizzy's treacherous front steps, Holly linked arms with her. The street was deserted, and the dogs ran frolicking in the snow. The plowed street was an ice rink. Halfway through the intersection, Holly lost traction, sliding before her feet flew into the air. She landed on her bottom, pulling Lizzy down with her. The two of them sat in the road, unable to stop laughing. One would stop and look at the other and it would start again. Mavis, growing impatient, barked twice. "Okay puppy. I hear you. Are you all right Holly?"

"I'm fine but I don't know if I can get up. It's so slick."

"Crawl toward the curb. We can walk in the snow."

They were still laughing when they entered Holly's house. Her father and Jason looked toward the door in surprise, Jason's expression changing to one of amusement when he caught sight of Lizzy's dark green sweater covered in red bows and glitter.

⁕⁕⁖⟳⬥⟲⁖⁕⁕

Lizzy was amused as well, and glad things weren't awkward between them. He was wearing an ugly sweater too, his covered in jingle bells and small candy canes. She smiled and gave him a little wave as she followed Holly toward the kitchen. Christmas carols and the smell of turkey greeted her as they passed through the dining room. The long, wooden table with its Christmas runner and fine China, was decorated with candles and laden with food.

The turkey sat on a platter in the kitchen, golden brown and perfect. Making gravy in the roasting pan, Mrs. Schneider smiled as they entered. "Are you girls hungry?"

"I'm suddenly starving," Lizzy said. "Everything smells delicious."

"Call your father to the table and ask Jason to come get the bird."

Holly left Lizzy in the kitchen and went to do as she was told.

"How long have you guys been cooking? You should have asked me to help," Lizzy said.

"Holly and I have been making holiday meals together for years. We have a system. Plus, we had Sage on hand." Mrs. Schneider smiled again and nodded toward Mrs. Fickle, who was sitting quietly at the kitchen table with a glass of wine.

Lizzy hadn't even noticed her. *I didn't get her a gift. What should I do? Maybe Holly can help me think of something.* Jason entered the kitchen to transport the turkey. Everyone got settled around the table and Lizzy was fully present in the moment.

Seated between Holly and Jason, her senses full, she tried to concentrate as they joined hands and Mr. Schneider said grace. He thanked God for sending his son to save them from their sins. Then he expressed gratitude for his family and friends and for the opportunity to celebrate Christmas together. Although they had danced together twice, something about holding Jason's hand at the dinner table felt intensely intimate. Lizzy's head swam in response to the scent of roast turkey. Everyone said, "Amen," and Jason gave her hand a squeeze, pulling her out of her trance. Mr. Schneider lifted his wine glass and was joined by everyone else. "Merry Christmas," he said.

"Merry Christmas."

Lizzy took several gulps of her wine then waited as the food was passed around. Turkey, stuffing, mashed potatoes, gravy, green beans with almonds, yams, cranberry Jello, salad, rolls; her plate was piled high with delectables. "My eyes might be bigger than my stomach."

"Don't forget to save room for pie," Holly said.

Jason looked at Lizzy's plate and chuckled. "There's no way."

After dinner, Lizzy helped with the dishes and was whisked off to the candlelight service at the Schneiders' church. She had never been to church and wasn't sure what to expect. Light blazed from the windows of the stone edifice. Bells rang through the frozen air and townsfolk approached from all directions, singly and in groups. Inside, Saint Timothy's was decorated with a tree and dozens of healthy-looking poinsettias. Friends and family greeted each other on the way to their seats, the sound of their voices echoing through the stone sanctuary. Glancing around, Lizzy asked Holly where Jason was.

"He was called to the station. He'll join us as soon as he can."

At seven o'clock, the bells ceased their ringing, and the organist began playing the prelude. The echo of the pipe organ in the stone structure gave Lizzy goosebumps. "What is this music?"

"It's from Handel's Messiah," Holly said. "It's beautiful, isn't it?"

She nodded.

When the music stopped, a group of children approached the front. Dressed in costumes which Holly said were used every year, they enacted the story of Mary and Joseph and the birth of baby Jesus. The story paused in places for the congregation to sing. The pastor gave a brief sermon about the meaning of Christmas, then handed the service over to the music director.

Jason slipped into the pew next to Lizzy as the carols began and volunteers passed out small candles with round cardboard drip protectors. People on either side of the aisle lit each other's candles and once all of them were lit, the congregation stood and made a circle around the outer perimeter. The lights went out. Standing in the dark with their candles, they sang a song Lizzy didn't know but she listened and enjoyed the sound of Jason's baritone voice beside her.

After the service, he asked if he could see her home. "We should talk," he whispered.

"Okay. When do we exchange presents?"

"I'll tell you the plan once we get to your house."

"Where are the dogs?"

"You'll see."

"So mysterious." She smiled. Leaning back in the passenger's seat, Lizzy closed her eyes and thought about her day. "I liked your family's Christmas. I think I'd like to do that every year."

Jason pulled up in front of her house and said, "Ready?"

"For what?"

"You'll see."

Lizzy got out of the cruiser and turned toward her house, then stopped, confused. "Is that a tree inside my window?"

"It kind of looks like it. Why don't we go investigate?"

Sprinting through the snow, Lizzy flung open her front door and stared. Between the roaring fire and the front window stood a large, decorated Christmas tree, with a star and tinsel and everything. Tears rolled down her cheeks.

"What's wrong?" Jason asked. "Don't you like it?"

"I didn't think I wanted a tree. I've never had one. But it's beautiful and I love it."

He wrapped her in a hug, and she turned toward him, pressing her face against his chest.

"There's more," he whispered.

"What else could there be?"

He led her through the house, pointing out the garland along the stair rail, the kitchen towels, the small artificial tree in her bedroom, even a Christmas-themed mouse pad.

"How?"

"Holly let me in, and I had some friends help me. That's why I was late."

"I'm sorry I was so mean last night. And you went to all this trouble anyway."

"Why don't you take your coat off and we'll sit by the fire."

When they sat, Lizzy noticed Mavis and Harvey laying in front of the fire. Mavis looked up at her and thumped her tail.

"I think I understand how you felt, maybe you still do?"

"I'm still frightened, but I've decided to stay."

"I hope you know that I wasn't trying to hurt you. I had no way of knowing about your past; we were just following protocol."

"I know. I just panicked. First Dottie and her friends knew and then I found out you'd talked to the Phoenix police. I felt like my world was crashing down around me."

"We'll all do our best to keep any reporters away from you. Even with all of the gossip and small grudges, this is a close-knit community and you're one of us now."

"Thanks."

"Would you feel better if I stayed on the sofa again? It's pretty cheerful in here."

"I'd like that. What about the presents? I see mine are under the tree."

Grinning, Jason said, "Everyone is coming over here tomorrow for breakfast and exchanging gifts. I didn't want to tell you before because I knew you'd say something about not having a tree."

"I don't have food either."

"Don't worry about that. It'll magically appear."

"I forgot about Mrs. Fickle. I didn't get her anything."

"She'll have plenty of presents to open. Do you still have the extra blanket and toothbrush?"

"You bet'cha."

"What? Where'd you learn that?"

"Hanging out with the locals." Lizzy waggled her eyebrows.

Chapter 25

Merry Christmas!

Waking to the sound of barking dogs and Christmas music, Lizzy felt excited to experience more of the Schneider family holiday. *I'm beginning to understand.* It was a season of firsts. *I wonder what I'm supposed to wear today.* She had no idea, so she threw on a pair of black jeans and a red sweater and headed down the stairs.

Following the scents of coffee and bacon, she passed the glowing Christmas tree and found everyone gathered in the kitchen. Holly was making eggs, and her mother was flipping pancakes. Mavis and Harvey were sitting patiently at Mrs. Schneider's feet, watching her every move. "Have a seat," she said. "It's almost ready."

"Maybe I should get a dining table. I've never had this many people over all at once."

"This is perfect. You have six chairs. We can just dish everything out over here so we'll all fit."

"You and Holly make a great team. She said she'll teach me how to cook so maybe next year I can help."

"Yay!" Holly said. "Come and get it."

They jostled around and filled their plates, then sat to eat at Lizzy's kitchen table. Six was a bit of a squeeze, but they managed. "Everything is delicious," Lizzy said. "What's in these pancakes?"

Holly giggled. "Remember when I told you I'm the only one who doesn't like candy canes? Mom keeps a couple plain ones out for me."

"Don't feed them to the dogs," her mother said. "Peppermint is bad for them."

After breakfast they moved into the living room and sat around the tree.

Jason played Santa and handed out presents one at a time, starting with the dogs. They each got a new rawhide bone. Holly gave Lizzy her own copy of her favorite cookbook and her first *ugly Christmas sweater*.

"For next year," she said.

When she opened her gift from Lizzy, she cried.

"What is it?" her mother asked, craning to see over her shoulder.

A tiny meow came from inside the box. "How did you know? I've never told anyone." She carefully removed a tiny white ball of fur and snuggled it to her chest.

"I have my methods," Lizzy said smugly.

"Ethel did say you were a witch." Holly giggled. She turned the kitten over and checked her underside. "I'll call her Candy and at Christmas we can give her a red bow. I love her. Thank you so much, Lizzy."

She didn't have a present from Jason, which reminded her of William. Brushing that memory away, she thought, *We don't really know each other that well so it's understandable*. When he got to her gift, he examined the packaging before slowly opening it. When he finally saw what it was, his eyes widened. He removed the elk antler and turquoise skinner knife from its leather sheath and studied it from every angle. "You must be a witch. This is the perfect gift. Thank you."

After they finished opening their presents, Mrs. Schneider went to the kitchen to make a batch of her famous peppermint hot chocolate and Jason pulled Lizzy aside, handing her a small package. "You didn't think I forgot about you?"

"I did, actually." She ripped the wrapping paper off and opened the rectangular box. Nestled inside, was a necklace. Her eyes glistened.

"Is it the right one?"

"You read my book?"

Jason nodded.

The necklace was like the one her main character, Rachel always wore for luck. An intricate silver dragon wrapped around a nephrite jade stone. It was as beautiful as she had imagined it. Her bottom lip quivered. "This is the nicest gift anyone has ever given me."

"I'm glad you like it."

"I more than like it. It's incredibly thoughtful," she said, then gave him a quick kiss on the cheek.

"Cocoa's ready," Mrs. Schneider called.

Fastening the clasp around her neck, Lizzy said, "Thank you."

"And thank *you* for the knife. It's amazing."

Once everyone but Holly had left, Lizzy sat with her on the sofa and watched the fire. Holly held Candy in one hand, against her chest. "She's so tiny. Has she even been weaned?"

Mavis climbed over Lizzy and gave Candy a sniff.

Her mother died in childbirth and the owners have been feeding her formula with an eyedropper. They gave me instructions and supplies. I thought you would be the perfect new mommy for her.

"I still don't know how you figured out that I secretly wanted a kitten, or how you managed to pick the perfect one. But she is the best present anyone could have given me. I'm so happy."

"I could explain how I figured it out, but then some of the magic and mystery would be gone." Lizzy smiled. "When are we going to take my new cookbook for a test drive?"

"Soon. But maybe not today. I've spent the past two days cooking, and I need a break."

"Is that cranberry Jello recipe in the cookbook?"

"No, that's a family recipe. I'll write it out for you if you want it."

"Out of all the food we ate, I think that was my favorite. What's in it?"

"A can of whole cranberries, cherry Jello, sour cream, celery, and walnuts. It sounds weird but everybody loves it. We always have to make a double batch."

"Sweet and tart, smooth and creamy with a crunch. It's a great palate cleanser too, when you're eating a savory meal."

"And it turns out you like peppermint."

"With chocolate. Yum."

"But you liked the pancakes too, didn't you?"

Lizzy grinned. "Maybe I'll fit in after all."

Staring into the fire she said, "My best gift was experiencing a real Christmas with people who care about me. I never understood why Christmas is such a big deal. I rolled my eyes at songs like Home for the Holidays or It's beginning to look a lot like Christmas. I thought they were just marketing ploys, but I get it now. And next year I'll be humming those songs and drinking peppermint cocoa while I decorate my tree.

"That's a gift for me too, because I need a partner in crime. Have you ever watched *Christmas Vacation*?"

"I don't think so."

"Grab a bottle of wine and get ready to laugh. You're going to love this."

Be the lovely who
Kindly leaves a review

Thank you so much for reading.

Booksellers may purchase multiple copies of this
book at a discount from IngramSpark.

Mother of two, cat mom, and prolific reader, Alice Kanaka is the author of eight mystery novels, numerous short stories, and a twelve-episode collaboration with Black Knight, author of the *Starshatter* space opera series.

Alice holds a bachelor's degree in Spanish and a Master of Business Administration with a concentration in Human Resources. She spent twelve years working at a state psychiatric hospital, speaks three languages, and has lived in seven countries.

A life-long fan of the mystery genre, Alice's books combine traditional tropes with contemporary characters to create whodunits that are simultaneously familiar and unique. Her aspiration is to write books that she would enjoy reading; stories that are both entertaining and uplifting, perfect with a cup of Earl Grey and a roaring fire on a gloomy day.

HTTPS://AliceKanaka.com